For Mom

Here Ghost Nothing

A Paranormal Cozy Mystery

Dina Marie

Copyright © 2024 by Dina Marie

All rights reserved.

No part of this publication may be reproduced, distributed, or transmitted in any form or by any means, including photocopying, recording, or other electronic or mechanical methods, without the prior written permission of the publisher, except as permitted by U.S. copyright law.

This is a work of fiction. Certain public figures and/or long-standing institutions, agencies, and public offices are mentioned, but the characters involved are wholly imaginary. Any similarity between the characters and/or situations to actual persons, living or dead, and/or actual events is unintentional and coincidental.

ISBN: 978-1-964858-15-9 (large-print paperback)

ISBN: 978-1-964858-16-6 (large-print hardcover)

Book cover design by Elizabeth Mackey

Chapter 1

I stood impatiently at my front door, looking at my watch.

He was late.

Across the driveway, Mr. Wiggins's door was open, some lighthearted chuckling coming from inside. Mrs. Birchgirdle was visiting Mr. Wiggins today, and from what I could see, they were involved in a pretty competitive game of Rummy. And it smelled as though Mr. Wiggins had made his famous chicken tortellini soup. The two of them looked so cute in there. Like a scene from *Up*.

"Well, hello, Clara!"

Ah, finally!

Charlie, the mailman, smiled when he saw me. "Do you think today might be the day?"

I had been waiting for Charlie each day, for the past few days, hoping he had a package for me. So far, he had only brought me bills. Advertisements, political literature, and bills. And more letters from Allison's attorney. (My sister-in-law was as tenacious as my husband, Joe, had been.) Fighting to keep my old, historic home was going to cost a pretty penny, but as far as I was concerned, it was worth every cent.

Charlie walked toward Mr. Wiggins's mailbox and inserted his mail. The clink of the lid attracted Mr. Wiggins's attention.

"Hi there, Charlie! Oh, hello, Clara! Lovely to see you."

"Hi, Mr. Wiggins!" I called as Charlie waved hello. "Mrs. Birchgirdle!"

When Charlie came toward me, he made a dramatic sweep through his mailbag. "Hmmm ... let me check."

Charlie was a cool mail carrier. The guy who delivered our mail on Long Island was creepy and nosy and didn't much care about being social (which was good because he probably had been a spy for Joe, so I shouldn't have been saying much to him anyway). But Charlie was different. When he introduced himself last week, he practically told me his life story: born and raised in Salem, married his childhood sweetheart, had newborn twins at home. I liked him immediately.

"Ta-da!" Charlie pulled out a small box. "I believe this is for you!"

It came! "Thank you, Charlie!"

"Seems like something special."

"Not really." I shrugged. "But it's special to me."

"Well, then it *is* special." He smiled and began walking out of the driveway. "Have a nice day!"

"You too!" I called and ran into the house, closing the door.

"It's here! It's here!" I called as Boy dropped my blond wig from his mouth and came running.

Bark!

"Sorry, sweetie, nothing for you today. This one is for momma."

William's ghostly form appeared in the kitchen. "Are those—"

"Yes!" I squealed, ripping open the small box and pulling out one of my first-ever business cards. "Look, William!" I showed it to him.

He looked it over. "Kensington House Bed-and-Breakfast. Your historic home away from home. Salem, Massachusetts. Proprietor: Clara Kelly." He looked at me with his pale blue eyes. "It's quite lovely."

"Business cards aren't as important as they used to be since so many business dealings are done online, but I thought I'd put them here so guests could grab them when they arrived." I pointed to a shelf on the antique cabinet across from the front door. "Also, since I'll be attending tonight's meeting of the Salem Small Business Group, I figured it was a good idea to start networking—you know, hand them out like a real businessperson."

"You *are* a true businessperson, Clara."

"Well, I don't really feel like it. We're not open yet. How did you solicit business in the eighteen hundreds?"

William shrugged. "As a cobbler, I truly never had the need. Those in Salem knew whom to contact when they needed a new sole."

I smiled. That description made William sound more like a priest than a shoemaker. "They call that word-of-mouth advertising."

"Aptly named," William said.

I ran my fingers across the face of the business card. "I know I'm still setting up all the legal stuff for the bed-and-breakfast, but this makes it seem real. Like it's really happening."

I placed the box of business cards on the dining table, which had become a dumping ground of sorts. Paint chips. Legal paperwork. Referrals from kind, old Mr. Wiggins for handymen, painters, floor care companies, carpet installers, accountants, lawyers. He had drawers full of names and numbers for any need or emergency. *Now, you had better treat her right*, he had warned a painter he recommended who had stopped by to give an estimate. He was protective. Not like Joe. In a good way. Like my father had been.

I flipped through the rest of the mail. "Well, we've gotten our first electric bill. How exciting! *Not.*" I ripped open the envelope and unfolded the bill as William read over my shoulder. "It doesn't seem so bad, right?"

"Does that denote the annual price?" he asked.

"No, it's for only one month."

William gasped. It reminded me of something a silent-movie actor might have made—with no audible breath—but it was a gasp nonetheless. Dramatic but soundless.

"And just think, when we start having guests and the electricity is used more, the bill will be even more than this." I laughed. "Something to look forward to."

William kept reading. "It says payment is due on June seventh."

"Yeah, we have time. That's the day after tomorrow."

"That is the date of my birth."

Now it was *my* turn to gasp. "William Kensington! Your birthday is June seventh?"

"Yes, is that of some significance?"

"Of course it is! We have to celebrate!"

"Why?"

"*Why?* Didn't you ever celebrate your birthday? Wasn't that a thing in the eighteen hundreds?"

"I didn't think it was cause for celebration."

"You mean you didn't have any parties when you were a kid?"

"Should I have?"

"Of course!" I thought of my own birthdays. Of my mom's happy face as she sat beside me and I gazed at the oversized, lopsided birthday cake she had made me. Of my dad taking a gazillion photos. *Hmmm...* I wondered where all those photos were. Probably buried in some closet in my dad's bedroom. Or in the attic. One of these days, I had to clean out my father's house, which was sitting empty on Long Island. "Birthdays are an American tradition, William. We celebrate every one."

"*Every* one?"

"Yes, *every one*. Sometimes with a party, especially if it's a big one like fifty or sixty. But even if there's no party, we like to recognize the passing of another year, another trip around the sun, as they say."

"Seems to me that it gives importance to something that is, well, insignificant."

"Well, I don't think your birthday is insignificant. And we will celebrate it with something special. You can count on it."

"Count on what?"

I smiled. "Never mind." I looked down at the business card in my hands. "I'm kinda nervous about tonight. Do I look like a businessperson?" I had already changed my clothing three times and had settled on a pair of jeans with no rips (which was surprisingly hard to find) and a black shirt and jacket.

"Very much so, Clara."

I was sure I looked like some kind of laborer in William's eyes—since, in his day, women wore mostly corsets, petticoats, and dresses—but he was always so kind. "What do *you* think?" I asked Boy, who had been gnawing on a bone. He looked up at me when he heard his name.

Bark!

I looked for Ghost Cat to see if she had an opinion, but she wasn't around. Probably off plotting ways to annoy her Shih Tzu brother. Or world domination.

"Thanks for the vote of confidence, guys."

I took a deep breath and stared at the word *proprietor* on the business card. Tonight was another first. If coming to Kensington House had marked the beginning of my new life, attending my first business function marked the beginning of my new career. And I needed all the positivity I could get.

Chapter 2

The Salem Small Business Group met in one of the downstairs rooms of the Salem Public Library. As I walked through the front doors, I remembered the last time I had been there. Not the best memory. When I had learned about William's past—how history viewed him as a traitor, a *notorious figure*, as one book title referred to him. But William was *not* a traitor. The textbooks were wrong. And that Mavis at the Salem Historical Society had been wrong, too. William was more of a patriot than anyone knew. He had killed Nathan Newbury in self-defense and had served the Union army honorably. And I was determined to clear his name.

I just hadn't figured out how yet.

I hurried down the stairs to the lower level, eager to begin my new career, but I froze. Men and women were mingling near the door to the assigned room, all looking so professional in their business-casual khaki pants, polo shirts, comfy blazers, and floral dresses. *I thought jeans were considered business-casual. At least, that was what a quick online search had told me. Had the rules changed while I was taking a shower?*

I took a deep breath and pushed myself toward the door, smiling sheepishly at the men and women standing there. Inside were about thirty people, all looking like they knew one another, all looking like they knew what they were doing. I wasn't sure what to do or where to go. I suddenly had the urge to curl up on the couch with a book from my library, with Boy snoring softly beside me.

"Hey, it's Clara, right?!"

Stephanie Hastings of Triple H Touring Company was coming toward me. A friendly face. And, even better, she was wearing jeans, like me. *Phew! Maybe I'm not a total impostor.* "Are you attending this evening's meeting of the Salem Small Business Group?" she asked.

"I think so. I've never been here before, so I'm not sure what to do. I'm a little nervous."

"Don't be silly! We're a helpful and generous bunch. Come on in. You can sit with me."

As I followed Stephanie and calmed my racing pulse, I realized I *did* know a few people in the large room. On the far right was Sissy Marshall, the owner of Haute Chocolate, who was grabbing a cup of coffee. Devon Derby, owner of Derby's Downtown Market, was seated in the front row, talking to Gladys, the owner of Bow-wow, Bones & Biscuits, the place that sold me all that overpriced stuff for Boy. I wondered if that was a technique she had learned here at the group (buy low, sell high!).

And across the room, Alice from The Haunted Cookie had her nose buried in a book, which wasn't surprising. I hadn't expected to see Alice mingling. She seemed like the shy and quiet type. I was surprised she was here at all, but for a girl who kept to herself, I seemed to run into her in a lot of places.

"We can sit here, right in front," Stephanie said.

I didn't want to tell Stephanie that I was more of a last-row kind of girl who ducked out if and when my anxiety got the best of me, but it was time to try something different. Maybe the new me would be a front-row girl. Stranger things had happened in the past few months!

Just as I was about to sit down, I heard, "Clara!"

I knew that voice.

And the green eyes that were attached to it.

I turned. "Sebastian! Hi!"

Sebastian looked cuter than usual. I didn't want to notice, but it was hard not to. I had become accustomed to seeing him full of dog hair, but he was wearing a pair of hair-free gray khakis, a matching T-shirt, and a pair of loafers. "It's so nice to see you here," he said.

"Well, I figured if I'm going to run a business in Salem, I need to get to know other businesspeople in town." I gestured toward Stephanie. "Do you know Stephanie?"

"Yes, Stephanie and I know one another."

"Yeah, I would call it *knowing one another*," Stephanie said with a laugh.

"Am I missing something?" I asked.

"We dated for a while," Stephanie said.

A tinge of jealousy swept through me, filling me with surprise. Only because that meant I liked Sebastian more than I was admitting to myself. Jealousy was a feeling I was familiar with and had lived with for many years. Jealous of the women I saw on the beach who could wear a bikini and not have their husbands think they were flirting with every guy on the sand. Jealous of the couples who had laughed easily in a restaurant, while I had to watch every word I said on the off-chance Joe would needlessly take offense. I was through with jealousy. At least, I wanted to be. *Go away!* I was here for one thing. To jumpstart my career. And I was doing it from the front row! Look at me!

Sebastian's cheeks reddened. "Yeah, Steph and I dated after college for a few months but thought we were better as friends."

"We're *totally* better as friends." Stephanie smiled and whispered to me, "Don't worry."

I wondered what that meant, but I didn't have time to ponder as Sebastian asked, "Do you mind if I join you?"

"Of course not," I said as Sebastian took the seat next to me.

As I put my things under my chair, Sissy from Haute Chocolate went to the front of the room.

"All right, everyone, we're going to get started," she said into a microphone.

"Is Sissy the president of the Salem Small Business Group?" I asked.

"Yeah. She was voted in a few months ago," Stephanie said. "She's great. Super organized and professional."

Sissy had her long, super-curly gray hair pulled back in a ponytail, so I could see her face. She must have been in her early sixties, judging by the laugh lines near her mouth and eyes, but she looked so young and vivacious. Maybe that was what selling chocolate did for a person.

"Welcome, everyone. Welcome! I'm happy to see you all here, and happy to see a few new faces." She nodded at me. "If you decide what you hear and see today is for you, we'd be happy to have you become an official member of the Salem Small Business Group. For those of you who don't know, we've been around for about twenty-five years, around the time that the world thought we would self-destruct because of Y2K." She laughed. "But I don't think many of you were around then—or you were too young to remember."

"I was only eight years old," Stephanie whispered.

"Me too," I said.

"Young 'uns." Sebastian waved a dismissive hand. "I was a very mature nine-year-old boy."

I giggled.

"Okay," Sissy continued. "A few housekeeping items before we get to the topic of today's meeting, How to Legally Collect Data on Your Customer, which is being presented by our guest speaker, Julia Samuels of the Salem-based Beta Data Corp." She motioned to a bright-eyed woman in the front row across the aisle from where we were sitting.

I wondered how soon I needed to start collecting data.

"If you're wondering how soon you need to begin collecting data on your customer, the answer is now," Sissy said. "No matter where you are in your business development."

Well, that answers that.

"On that business development note," Sissy continued, "it's time for our annual trip, and this year, we're organizing a group to take next month to Las Vegas for a conference titled Business Start-Up 101: Everything You Wanted to Know About Starting a Business and Were Afraid to Ask."

A trip? *To Las Vegas?* I had always wanted to go to Las Vegas. It seemed so glamorous and exciting. Plus, there was plenty I wanted to know about starting a business and was afraid to ask. "Are either of you going on this trip?" I whispered.

"Yeah, Sissy mentioned it to me last week," Stephanie said. "It's definitely for me. What about you, Sebastian?"

"Can't," he said. "I'm booked solid for the next six weeks. I can't let those doggies down."

"That's a good problem to have," I said. "A full calendar of steady business."

"You're not kidding. It wasn't always that way. Which is why—as much as I'd like to go to Vegas and play a few games of craps—I need to stay here. You should go, though, Clara. I can watch Boy for you."

"Awww, thank you." It was kind of him to offer. I hadn't even thought about having to board Boy anywhere. I figured he could stay home with William. But how was I supposed to explain that I was leaving my dog with my ghost roommate?

"If you're interested, we'll be taking a group of six, including myself and, I believe, Stephanie Hastings, right, Stephanie?"

"Count me in, Sissy!" Stephanie called.

"It's a good opportunity for those of you just starting your business to learn some of the basics, but it's also good for others to review business practices and learn a few tricks. The group will cover your conference fee, but you're on the hook for your flight and hotel stay. Not a bad deal. See me afterward if you're interested." She looked at her notes. "And one last item before I introduce Julia. We have two sponsorships left for Kai Teller's *Here Goes Nothing* event that's taking place at the Wyatt House tomorrow night."

There were a few groans in the audience.

"All right, all right," Sissy said. "I know some of us are not keen on the idea of our little Salem attracting so much attention. And I know we like our small town to remain just that—small. But remember, tourism is a big part of what many of our businesses need to survive. Personally, my sales at Haute Chocolate skyrocket in the Halloween season—I'm talking ten times the average—and I'm sure many of you can say the same, so we are going to embrace Kai Teller and his legions of fans."

"Who's Kai Teller?" I whispered to Stephanie.

Before she could answer, Sissy said, "For those of you who don't know who Kai Teller is ..." *Okay, was chocolate maven Sissy Marshall also a mind reader?* "... he's a YouTuber known for doing all kinds of stunts for his web show, *Here Goes Nothing*, and he likes to partner with local businesses and give them the opportunity to get their products and services in front of his fans—which number in the millions, by the way. He's kind that way. And tomorrow night, he has decided he is going to spend the night alone in a," she said these next two words with air quotes, "*haunted house*. If he *survives* the night ..." More air quotes. "... he'll be donating a million dollars to the Feeding Salem local charity." There were a few oohs and aahs in the audience. "Like I said, he's kind that way. I'll come around with the brochure if anyone is interested."

"Clara, what's the matter?" Stephanie asked. "You look a bit pale."

"Did she say *haunted house*?"

"You don't believe in ghosts, do you?" Sebastian asked.

"Um..."

"Wyatt House is one of the most popular stops on my Hauntings Tour," Stephanie said. "It's an old building with a bit of a disturbing history and looks pretty spooky, so it attracts a lot of attention."

Did she say *disturbing history*? I was pretty sure Mavis at the Salem Historical Society thought Kensington House had a disturbing history, too. "Have you ever seen any paranormal activity there?" I asked.

"Some of the guests who've taken my tour have said they've seen a ghost roaming the upper floor. A woman named Beth Wyatt lived in the house in the seventeen hundreds, and a thief entered her home one night looking to steal some jewelry and knocked over the baby bassinet. Her baby died from his injuries."

"That's terrible," I said.

"As the story goes," Stephanie said, "Beth, understandably, never recovered. A few months later, she took her own life. Legend has it that she is spending eternity seeking revenge on the thief, who was never found."

Sebastian gave a little laugh. "People believe what they want to believe."

"Says the skeptic," Stephanie said with a giggle.

"I've lived in Salem all my life," Sebastian said, "with the exception of the four years I went to Boston University, and I have yet to see a ghost."

Okay, so Sebastian couldn't see ghosts. I still didn't know why *I* could.

"That said, I think you should put in for the sponsorship, Clara," he said.

"Me? But I barely have a business yet. At this point, I have a name. Kensington House. And a pocketful of business cards." *Still untouched in my back pocket, by the way.*

"All the more reason," Sebastian said. "I follow Kai Teller's adventures, and wherever Kai goes, his multitudes of fans follow. It's going to look like Halloween here tomorrow night in Salem. Expect crowds. It's never too early to start marketing, to start spreading the word about Kensington House."

"It's a good idea, Clara," Stephanie said. "The sponsorships aren't crazy expensive. I bought one as well."

"What would I have to do?" I asked.

"Not much," Stephanie said with a shrug. "Write a check. Show up tomorrow night with a table and some marketing materials." *It already sounded like too much.* "Then show up again the next morning after Kai Teller miraculously survives his night in the haunted house, and then think about all the ways you're going to start marketing to your growing email list."

It might be a good idea. If Joe's sister, Allison, was contesting the inheritance, I'd need to start generating my own money and customer base fast.

Sissy appeared in front of us. "Anyone here interested in sponsoring *Here Goes Nothing* tomorrow night?"

"I am." I raised my hand.

"Great. You've got the last sponsorship, Clara. What's the name of your business?"

My throat constricted. My business? *Yes, I am a real businessperson.* "Kensington House Bed-and-Breakfast."

"Terrific. You can see me after the meeting, and we'll get everything squared away."

As Sissy returned to the front of the room, Stephanie nudged me. "Way to go, Clara. You're on your way."

I appreciated the sentiment, but I couldn't help but think: on my way to what?

When Sissy returned to her podium, she cleared her throat. "Congratulations to Alice of The Haunted Cookie and Clara of Kensington House Bed-and-Breakfast on securing the last two sponsorships for tomorrow night." The audience clapped, and I could feel my cheeks warm. "Again, moneys raised by Kai Teller's stunts always benefit a local charity, and, in this case, they will go to Feeding Salem, which, as many of you know, could really use the funding. Kai will be stopping by their downtown office before he gets to Wyatt House." More clapping. "Okay, now that housekeeping is done, I am thrilled to be able to introduce today's speaker …"

My mind was racing. Wow. I did a thing. My first public-facing thing. Kensington House was sponsoring a YouTuber. *Nineteenth century meets twenty-first century.* Fun. Now all I had to do was find myself a table and some marketing materials.

Chapter 3

Sebastian wasn't kidding.

There must have been hundreds of young people standing outside Wyatt House, chanting Kai Teller's name and waiting to get a glimpse of him when he arrived. As a kid, I had gone with my parents once to New York City's Times Square on New Year's Eve, and the mass of bodies out here tonight rivaled that shoulder-to-shoulder crowd, barricaded behind lines of police officers.

"I'm glad I'm in here and not out there," Stephanie said. She was standing next to me, peering out one of Wyatt House's front windows and nibbling on a cookie featuring Kai Teller's face on it in white cream.

"Me too," I said.

"Well, are you ready for your first business gig?"

"It feels weird."

"Yeah, it will in the beginning, but you'll get the hang of it. Just remember to have fun."

Stephanie grabbed another Kai Teller cookie from The Haunted Cookie's sponsor table, took a bite out of his head, and walked back to the far corner of the room where her table had tons of Triple H Touring Company brochures and swag.

Meanwhile, my sponsor table looked like I had just purchased it at Home Depot. (Which I had.) No bells and whistles. Just my business cards and a clipboard and pencil for people to join my mailing list, which I wasn't even sure what I was supposed to do with. So much for twenty-first century. I had been so focused on registering a domain name and throwing up a quick website that I had forgotten

I needed to look like I had a business in *real* life, too. That Las Vegas conference I had signed up for couldn't come soon enough. I needed all the help I could get.

I rubbed the goosebumps on my arms. Either it was a bit chilly in this old house or I was nervous about tonight. Possibly both. There was a third possibility, of course. That the chill was coming from the angry ghost of Beth Wyatt hovering around me and looking to avenge her baby's death. So far, I hadn't seen a ghost, and I was hoping that meant that Wyatt House was, indeed, drafty and not harboring a murderous specter.

I looked around. So much of Wyatt House reminded me of Kensington House. It had the same colonial charm (and also the same state of disrepair). From the floral wallpaper to the wainscot chests and chairs. Maybe the Wyatts and Kensingtons had the same interior designer.

A large sign from the Salem Historical Society was located on an easel near the front door.

Wyatt House

Wyatt House was one of the first period houses of Salem, Massachusetts. Originally built in 1675 by Roland Wyatt, a carpenter, the house was bequeathed to Roland's only son, Barnaby, when Roland died of smallpox in 1691.

Smallpox. Yikes. Whenever I wondered what William's life had been like in the eighteen hundreds, I never considered the diseases he could potentially be exposed to. Was smallpox still around in 1863? It was so easy to romanticize the past and complain about the present, but the truth was that modern medicine was a lifesaver. Literally.

Two years later, nineteen-year-old Barnaby wed Marion Godfrey, daughter of the local blacksmith, and together they had three children, including a son, John, who grew to be a carpenter like his grandfather. By the time John was eighteen years of age, his mother also died of smallpox, and his two sisters married and left Salem. In 1714, John added this first room to Wyatt House as well as the second story. Originally intending this room to be an open front porch, John decided to enclose it so that he and his longtime sweetheart and soon-to-be wife, Beth Clark, could use it as an extra room as they both desired to have a large family.

I could almost envision John and Beth Wyatt sitting in this room in rocking chairs, bouncing babies on their knees. The sign went on to say that the Salem Historical Society would begin work in the next six months to renovate Wyatt House, which would be used as part of the architectural curriculum at the University of Massachusetts.

How nice to think that this old house would be full of students one day, learning about its history.

I walked toward the partial wall that separated this room from the main area of the house—a large room with old furniture pushed to the side. A *Here Goes Nothing* social media wall, which looked out-of-place in this centuries-old home, had been erected in the center. In front of it, an air mattress with a photo of Kai Teller's face printed on the top cushion had been set up, along with a few tables that had snacks and a few books. I assumed this would be where Kai Teller would perform his stunt tonight.

My stomach grumbled. I had spent so much time on the computer at the library today, figuring out how to set up a website, that I had forgotten to eat. I picked up a Kai Teller cookie from The Haunted Cookie's table, which looked like it had been decorated by a team from the Food Network. There were neat rows of Kai Teller cookies as well as cookies in the shapes of ghosts and witches, and several wicker baskets of magnets in the shape of donuts and imprinted with *The Haunted Cookie* in what looked like powdered sugar. All atop a white tablecloth with a multicolored sprinkle design. Alice, who was standing at the other end of her table and inspecting her fingernails, may have been a quiet one, but she clearly knew what she was doing. She was even wearing her apron, like she was about to begin recording a baking podcast. She looked up and caught my eye, and I waved.

"Hi, I don't think we've officially met," I said. "I stopped in The Haunted Cookie once, and I've seen you a few places, but I'm not sure if you remember me."

"I remember you," she said in a timid voice.

Is that good or bad? "My name is Clara Kelly." I popped the rest of Kai Teller's face into my mouth and stuck out my hand.

"Alice Sutton." She reached across the table to shake it. Her hand was small and slipped into mine easily.

"This is exciting, isn't it?" I asked.

Alice shrugged like it was nothing special.

"These cookies are great, by the way." I pointed to my chewing mouth, as if I really needed to. "Who knew Kai Teller could be so delicious?"

Alice smiled and continued busying herself by securing her tablecloth to the table. I wanted to ask her if she was going to the Las Vegas business conference next month when a voice said, "Well, if it isn't Clara Kelly."

I turned around. Taylor Hampton from the *Salem Chronicle* was standing in front of my table, picking up one of my business cards. He looked up at me with his deep-set brown eyes, blowing the bangs off his forehead, and bent down to sign my mailing list. "Why don't you do this online or with a QR code or something?" he said, reaching for the pencil attached to the clipboard. "Whatever. I'll be your first name. This way, it doesn't look so empty."

What a guy. "Taylor, hi. What are you doing here?"

"I'm covering this event for the *Chronicle*," he said with an unspoken *duh*. "Kai Teller always gives an exclusive to the local newspaper when he does a stunt. Mabel said he asked for me by name." He said this with an air of pride and seemed to be expecting some kind of reaction from me.

"Oh, that's great," I said and suddenly had a thought. "You know, Taylor, I may have an interesting story for you."

Immediately, Taylor seemed bored by my pitch without even hearing it, and I asked myself, *Do you really want to ask for Taylor Hampton's help on this?* I figured I had to start somewhere. "It might be the biggest scoop of your career."

He reached for one of Alice's ghost cookies and looked at me. Now I had his attention. "Really? What is it?"

"Well, the house I moved into is known as Kensington House."

"Yeah, I can see that." He pointed to the handwritten sign I had taped to my pathetic-looking sponsor table.

"So you've heard of it?"

"Who hasn't?" He rolled his eyes.

"Well, that's just it. I know the house has a certain reputation and that William Kensington, the gentleman who lived in the house in the 1800s, was, according to the history books," I swallowed, "you know, a traitor and was hanged for treason, but I have it on good authority that isn't true." How exciting that I was going to get William exonerated! "William Kensington actually killed Nathan Newbury in self-defense!"

I didn't know if I expected a reaction from Taylor, but there was none. Other than a dramatic yawn. He reached for another ghost cookie and took a bite of it. I kept talking since I didn't know what else to do.

"What really happened was William Kensington discovered that Nathan Newbury was a southern sympathizer—or maybe in the Confederate secret service. He was working with others to infiltrate the Union army. *Nathan* was the traitor! And when Nathan realized that William knew what he was up to, he tried to kill him. Only William killed him first."

Taylor took his time chewing and then swallowing, his Adam's apple bobbing down and up. When he finished, he said, "On whose authority?"

"Excuse me?"

"You said you had it on good authority that what you're telling me is true."

Ugh. Road Block Number One. How was I supposed to tell him that my authority was the ghost of the guy who was hanged for treason? *Think of something.* "Well, as they say in journalism, I have to protect my sources."

"Well, as I say right now, you're not a journalist, and it doesn't work that way." He smirked. "*I* protect my sources. *You* don't. How it works is, you spill your guts to me, and I decide if your guts are worth pursuing."

"But what I'm telling you is true. Isn't that enough to make it worth pursuing?"

"Well, excuse me if I don't run to the *Chronicle*'s office and stop the presses because a woman I've seen talking to herself around town is convinced that the house she moved into did not belong to a traitor but a hero. Sounds to me like you're trying to change the profile of your house now that you've decided to open a bed-and-breakfast. Maybe boost your property value." He took another bite of his cookie. "It's not my fault that you didn't do your research on your house. You can't change history, Clara."

"I'm not *changing* history, Taylor. I'm just changing the way it's remembered."

"Seriously?" His deep-set brown eyes narrowed. "You're telling me every history book is wrong, and you're right? That I should believe *you*? Man, I knew you might be crazy, but I didn't think you were delusional." There was an uproar outside Wyatt House. "Sorry, gotta go. I've got things to cover in the *twenty-first* century, thank you."

As he glided away, I glanced at Alice, who had been watching our interaction. She quickly averted her eyes as if she might be blinded by looking at me. For some reason, I had the urge to eat another Kai Teller cookie. I grabbed one as the front door opened, and a young man with a neatly clipped mustache and beard walked in with a group of people, all of whom looked to be in their late twenties, with the exception of one middle-aged woman. I recognized the first young man immediately—from the cookie I held in my hand.

"I love you back!" Kai Teller was yelling to his legions of screaming fans outside Wyatt House as one of his buddies videoed him. "We got this! Thank you so much for coming!"

As soon as the door closed and the camera was turned off, he rolled his eyes. "Don't these people have jobs?"

So this is Kai Teller.

A young woman in a blue baseball cap directed Kai and his cohorts toward the sponsor tables, and I quickly got behind my Home Depot table to at least look somewhat professional. "Kai, these are the sponsors of tonight's event," she said.

"Thank you, Sam. Can't forget my sponsors!" But instead of coming to us individually and thanking us for supporting this little event, Kai waved at us with a grand, "Hello, sponsors!" Then he directed the guy with the phone camera to interview each of us for thirty seconds. "No more than thirty seconds, Justin," Kai said. "No need to overtax my storage. Start with the cookie lady and end with the redheaded lady."

Redheaded lady? *That was me.* I was being interviewed? How much could I say in thirty seconds? Had I remembered to brush my hair?

Taylor, who had been pushing his way toward Kai's inner circle, introduced himself. "Hi, Taylor Hampton, from the *Salem Chronicle*. Thank you for inviting me to be here."

"Terrific," Kai said, shaking Taylor's hand. "Nice to have you, Tommy."

"Um, it's—"

But Kai Teller was already moving into the house. "So this is the big, scary house I'm staying in tonight? Yo, Justin, I thought you said this place was creepy."

Justin, the guy who had been about to video Alice, pulled a lollipop out of his pocket. "Not so creepy. This'll be cake for you, Kai. Easiest stunt you ever pulled."

"Got that right. I can already feel my subscriber numbers going up."

The front door opened again, and I expected another twenty-something member of Kai Teller's entourage to appear, but in walked Mavis from the Salem Historical Society. I had to do a double-take. She was the last person I thought I would see at a YouTuber event. Even more surprising? Beverly, the gossiping cashier from Derby's, walked in right behind her. I had forgotten the two were best buddies. Or so said Mavis when I had spoken to her at the Salem Historical Society.

"Can I help you, old timer?" Kai asked when Mavis walked in.

"Old timer?" Mavis raised her drawn-on eyebrows.

"This is Mavis Simpson from the Salem Historical Society, Kai," Sam, the young woman in the baseball cap, said.

"Oh, that's right, Sam. Totally forgot." He greeted Mavis. "I appreciate you, Mavis. Thanks for coming. Right this way."

Mavis looked unsure, and her eyes were checking out Alice's confectionery delights, but Beverly was egging her on, videoing her with her phone. "Go, Mavis, this will be great for my Insta feed."

Kai called out, "Justin, *let's goooo*. Turn it on, bro!"

"Oh, sorry." Justin, who had been browsing Stephanie's brochures, moved his lollipop to the other side of his mouth and hurried to Kai's side.

As soon as the camera was rolling, Kai Teller put on a big smile. "Yo, Kai Krew, I'm here at the Wyatt House in Salem, Massachusetts, for the next episode of your favorite YouTube show, *Here Goes Nothing*! Ready for my big night in a haunted house. Oooh, scary!" He pretended to bite his nails. "I'm here with my Kai Five. You know them all! They accompany me to all my events, but I'll give a quick intro for those who may be new to my channel." He pointed to the middle-aged woman he had arrived with. "This is my amazing mom, Linda."

"Love you, Kai!" She smiled big into the camera.

"And this is Sam, my personal assistant." The girl in the blue baseball cap waved. "I don't know what I would do without her." He moved on to two guys, a dark-haired young man whose long hair was pulled back into a man bun and a fair-skinned skinny guy with freckles. "And this is my main man Miltos, who's in charge of snacks." Man Bun gave a wave. "And this is Danny, who does crowd control. And then there's Justin behind the camera." Justin turned the camera on himself and waved before turning it back to Kai.

"And we have a special guest today," Kai said. "I've got Mavis Simpson here from the Salem Historical Society. Yo, Mavis, thanks for being here!"

Mavis pulled down on her pink button-down blouse, looking uncomfortable. I didn't blame her. Beverly stood nearby, taking photos with her own camera, like Mavis's personal paparazzi.

"Mavis ... is it okay if I call you Mavis?" Kai asked. Before Mavis could answer, he asked, "Can you tell us why you think this house is haunted?"

"I don't *think* it's haunted," she said with a roll of her eyes.

I was familiar with that condescending eye roll. It had been one of the first things I noticed about Mavis. I was beginning to think it was her calling card.

"I *know* it is," she continued. "I know *all* the homes that are haunted in Salem."

Not *all* of them.

"Well, how do you *know* it's haunted?" Kai asked.

"We've had many, many reports of paranormal activity in Wyatt House over the years," Mavis said with authority. "There are the usual signs. Creaking floors. Mysterious noises, like doors closing. Sudden drops in temperature. Dogs that seem to bark at nothing."

I felt seen.

"But we've also had reports of tourists entering Wyatt House and feeling ill. They're fine one minute, and then the next they have a headache or complain of feeling like someone is pinching them. Like pins and needles. The historical society has commissioned experts to come in and investigate, and their meters and other doohickeys have detected sudden changes in electromagnetic fields."

"Fascinating," Kai said, although I got the feeling he didn't think it was all that fascinating. "Does this haunting have to do with the Salem Witch Trials?"

"Not at all." Mavis gave another roll of her eyes as if the question were either dumb or distasteful. "Beth Wyatt, a woman who lived in this house in the early seventeen hundreds, took her own life after her infant son was killed during a burglary."

"Oooh ..." Kai said as Sam, the young woman with the baseball cap, shined a flashlight under his face and he looked into Justin's camera lens. "Spooky!"

Mavis didn't look enthused. "This is very serious. It is said that Beth Wyatt continues to haunt this old house, looking to get her revenge. I don't really think it's safe for you to be here alone. But no one in your organization asked for my opinion."

"Mavis, look into the camera when you talk," Beverly whispered.

Mavis cleared her throat and looked into Justin's camera. "I don't really think it's safe for you to be here alone."

"Well, that's a very cool story and thanks for the tip, Mavis." Kai motioned for Mavis to get out of his shot. She shook her head and obliged as he walked toward the middle of the room. "This is where I'll be spending the night." He waved his hands and spun around. "The Salem Historical Society people were kind enough to give us the run of the house, and we've promised to be good boys and girls and not disturb anything. Right, Mavis?"

Mavis looked confused, and Kai plowed on. "As you can see, I have all my supplies." He pointed to the table that had been set up in the room. "Potato chips. Sugared soda. Lots of cookies. The overnight meal of champions." Kai's posse cheered. "Here is my bed. My trusty air mattress—which is available in my store with my other merch. You may remember this mattress from the time I spent the night in the New York City subway system. If you don't, be sure to check out that video on my YouTube channel, and while you're there, don't forget to like and subscribe!" Another cheer from the Kai Five. "Well, as we like to say, here goes nothing! See you all tomorrow," Kai said, adding in a creepy voice, *"If I make it . . ."*

When the camera was off, Kai's cohorts gushed.

"You did awesome, Kai!"

"This will be the best stunt yet!"

"You get better with every show!"

Kai took all the compliments in stride. "Okay, people, listen up! Get some B-roll of this place so we can edit it all together this weekend. Justin, did you finish the sponsor interviews?"

"Um, Kai, I didn't get a chance. I was videoing you the entire time."

"Well, get on it. Remember, people, no one stays here tonight but me, and you don't come in. We'll see if this old house is haunted, after all. Let's *gooooo*, people!"

As Kai's people ran around to do his bidding, I mentally tried to figure out what I was going to say in my thirty-second sponsor video. I took out my phone and quickly did an online search. Website? Check. (Thank goodness for the library computers because designing even a rudimentary website on my phone was nearly impossible!) Mailing list? I looked down at my clipboard. Check. QR code? Um, I didn't have that. Online mailing list? I didn't have that either. Well, I knew how I was going to spend the rest of my night when I got home. Trying to figure out all these things on my phone. I really needed a computer. (Or a library that was open 24/7.)

"Sponsors, thank you so much for being here," Linda, Kai's mother, was saying. She was standing near the front door in a stylish flare-sleeve print top and wide-leg pants. "A quick announcement before Justin gets started. We have many more opportunities for sponsorships that don't require attendance at Kai's events. In other words, there are dozens of companies graciously sponsoring tonight's festivities from afar, which is why we are able to provide such a large charitable donation. I've left envelopes on your tables of the shows we have coming up, so you can see what we have planned. Note: the original contract you signed includes an NDA, non-disclosure agreement, and there is some proprietary stuff in those envelopes that is not for public consumption. You should know I take legal matters very seriously. Okay, Justin, carry on."

Justin hurried toward Alice's table, bumping into Beverly, who was browsing Alice's cookies with Mavis.

"You did great, Mavis," Beverly was gushing.

Mavis was basking in the glow of Beverly's praise, but when the two women saw me, they smiled politely, grabbed several more cookies, and whispered animatedly to one another as they walked out the front door.

"Smile, Clara!"

I barely turned around and smiled before a flash blinded me. When the bright spots began to go away, Stephanie handed me a still-developing Polaroid picture.

"Polaroids, huh?" I said, shaking the film to help it dry. "Very old school."

"Yeah, but the kids seem to love these nowadays," she said. "You know what they say. Everything old is new again."

Gosh, I hoped so. I would love for young people to take a chance on a historic bed-and-breakfast. "Would you like one of you?"

"Nah, I have plenty of me." She looked at Justin, who was finishing up with Alice. "Oops, gotta go. It's time for my video."

"Good luck!"

I straightened the clipboard on my sponsor table, as if that would help make it more professional instead of what it was. Pathetic. Then I stared at the developing Polaroid in my hands. My face came in first and then my red hair. Ugh. Not the best photo of me. But Stephanie got a great view of Alice and her picture-perfect table in the background. Even that guy Justin made the photo. The two of them looked way better than I did.

As I put the photo in my purse, Justin was finishing up with a guy who was a comic book store owner, whom I hadn't formally met, and hurried toward me. "Okay, you've got thirty seconds to tell Kai's millions of followers why they should care about your business. Ready, go." He held the camera phone in front of his face.

Panic. He wasn't wasting any time. *Keep it together.*

"Hi, my name is Clara Kelly, and I'm the proprietor of a new bed-and-breakfast here in

Salem called Kensington House. We're brand new. Under construction. But we'll be open for business this fall, just in time for the Halloween season." I took a quick breath. "We are conveniently located, offering quick access to downtown Salem and all the famous landmarks. We're competitively priced, and if you're driving, we have a driveway so you can park your car. I look forward to hosting you when you come to stay."

I began panting as if I had just run a marathon.

Justin turned off the camera and stuck another lollipop into his mouth while I tried to keep myself from hyperventilating. "Nice job," he said. "Have you done this kind of thing before? You were great."

"Thanks." My brain wanted to believe him, but my stomach was turning with anxiety.

"You know, I have my own show coming out next year. *Just Justin*. A day-in-the-life kind of thing. I can send you info on sponsorship ops."

"Um, sure." The thought of doing even more videos made my stomach turn even more.

"Good deal." He bit down on his lollipop. "Okay, we'll need you back here about six thirty a.m. That gives us time to group and get to Kai by seven a.m. Then the guy from Feeding Salem will be arriving just before nine o'clock, and Kai will be presenting the check for a million bucks. He likes to have the sponsors around him. He asks if you can wear blue."

"Blue?"

"He says it's his best color." Justin shrugged. "Do your best. Teal or something similar works, too."

"Okay, sponsors!" Kai was calling. "Once your video is done, you can skedaddle—and I'll see you all in the morning for the big donation. Thank you so much for the support! And Justin, don't forget to tell the Feeding Salem guy to bring a few kids with him tomorrow morning—the skinnier, the better!"

"Already taken care of, Kai!" Justin called as he hurried into the main room of the house.

"Way to go, Clara!" Stephanie was clapping and cheering. "You did a great job on your video. Like a pro."

I didn't feel like a pro. Especially from the rib cage down. "Is there a bathroom around here?"

"Are you okay?"

"I don't know." It was hard to believe I would get so nervous about a thirty-second video, especially since I felt like I was being watched 24/7 living with Joe for a whole eight years. "I guess I wasn't ready for my close-up."

"No working bathrooms in the place. I think there's a porta-potty outside, in the back of the house."

"Here." Alice handed me a bottle of water from her table.

"Thank you, Alice," I said, but she was already looking away. I turned to Stephanie. "I might head to the bathroom anyway. Maybe dab some of this water onto my face."

"Do you need me to stay?"

"No, I'll be fine. I'll see you in the morning."

"The bathroom is right over there." Stephanie pointed to the left side of the main room. "You better hurry, though. This Kai guy looks like he's anxious to be alone."

I sprinted toward the bathroom, bumping into Kai's friend Danny, who was charging toward the front door like a man on a mission, followed by Miltos, who was running after him.

"Um, you're going the wrong way, whoever you are!" Kai was shouting as I hurried toward an open door that I prayed was a bathroom.

"I'll just be a minute!"

I quickly closed the door and looked around. It *was* a bathroom. (Thank God.) There was an old-fashioned pedestal sink and a matching toilet, which had no water, but that didn't stop me from nearly vomiting into it. *What is wrong with me?* And then it hit me. *The camera.* Yes, I had lived with cameras on me for eight years. But maybe a camera shining directly on me again was reminding me of Joe's constant surveillance. I turned on the sink faucet, but when nothing came out, I poured some water from the bottle Alice had given me onto my hands. I was dabbing it onto my face when someone banged on the door, startling me. I opened it. Kai's personal assistant, Sam, was standing there.

"We gotta go," she said. "Everyone's cleared out. Are you okay?" She looked at my face with concern.

"I'm all right. I'll be right out. Just give me another minute."

I closed the door and looked at my reflection in the mirror above the sink. Sam was right. I didn't look too good. I looked gray. Like William. *Is this what business exposure does to me?* I'd never survive. I had better get my sea legs when it came to online marketing. Or *any* marketing. I was sure there would be a lot more videos in my future.

I took some deep breaths and was starting to feel a little bit better. Maybe it was the isolation. Or all the white tiles around me. My cheeks had cooled; my breathing had steadied. I would survive my first business event!

There was a small pile of paper towels on the sink. (I wasn't sure why. There was no water to soak up.) But I was grateful and pulled one off, drying my face. I was about to toss my paper towel into a tiny white wicker trash basket, but I didn't want to dirty it, so I shoved my trash into my pocket.

A knock on the door. Less frantic, but still loud.

When I opened it, Sam was standing there, the light of the bathroom making her look like an apparition. "We have to go," she whispered.

"Yeah, sorry. I'm ready."

The main room was completely dark now except for a line of candles that was surrounding Kai, who was still, turned over on his air mattress, his blankets over him. The scene looked like a funeral. Or a séance. Or both.

Quietly, Sam and I hurried toward the sponsors' room, which was also dark and quiet. No one manning the tables. My table didn't look so bad in the dark. *Maybe I should only do marketing events at night in houses where there is no electricity.* Sam held the door open for me.

"Did Justin tell you?" she asked. "We need to be here at six thirty a.m."

"Yes, I'll be here."

"Great, see you then."

As I stepped outside, the Kai Krew cheered, probably hoping to get one last glimpse of their fearless leader. When they saw me, disappointment covered their faces, and they put their phone cameras down. I couldn't believe so many of his fans were still here. Were they going to sleep here?

On the street? Nearby? Were they going to sleep at all?

I looked inside Wyatt House and at Kai, lying there in the dark under candlelight. Did he just wake up one day and think to himself, I'm going to make a living by having people crowdfund crazy stunts and then donate the proceeds to charity?

Well, someone had to do it, I guess.

And judging by the way I responded to any attention at all, it sure wasn't going to be me.

Chapter 4

Bark! Bark!

As I limped into Kensington House, a commotion greeted me. Boy was running in circles around the dining table, trying to get to Ghost Cat, who was curled on top with my blond wig. She was peering down at the dog in triumph.

"What are you two up to?" I tossed the shoe I had broken on the walk home next to the front door and reached out to scratch Ghost Cat's ears; she pushed her little head into my fingers. "Um, I don't think this belongs to you, you little rascal." I picked up the wig and threw it to Boy, who snatched it eagerly and ran into the living room. Ghost Cat looked at me blankly and began to lick her paw.

"Did you have a prosperous gathering, Clara?" William asked, appearing in the kitchen.

I shrugged. "Well, the walk home wasn't so successful." I pointed to my shoe. "My heel broke when I was about two blocks from home. Great. And as for my first business event, I'm not sure how prosperous it was. I was so busy designing a website—which is a good thing, I know—but my sponsor table was just not appealing. Who would want to visit a business with a lousy table?"

William looked at me with concern, although I'm sure he had no idea what I was talking about. "Table?"

"Here, let me show you. I took a few photos." I pulled out my phone and swiped from photo to photo. "This is Alice from The Haunted Cookie. Look how beautiful that table looks, with the tablecloth looking like a sprinkled donut with frosting that matches the color of her cookies. And this is Stephanie of Triple H Touring Company. Have you ever seen so many brochures? And look at this one. This is for a comic book store called Ghostly Ink. Look how colorful!"

William let me babble on and on, although he seemed more interested in my phone than what was on the screen. "May I?" he asked, using his gray pointer finger to swipe.

"Sure."

He touched his finger to the screen gingerly, as if afraid it might break. When he was able to swipe to the next photo, he looked pleased.

"I just wanted to make a good first impression," I said. "I'm not sure if I have. And the video they took?" I face-palmed. "Stephanie seemed to like it, but I don't remember a word I said."

William retracted his finger. "Clara, I've no doubt you fared quite well. We learn from our blunders and do better in the next go-round."

"The whole thing was kinda weird. We set up tables, but none of Kai's fans were allowed inside the house. It's like the sponsors did all that just to be featured in Kai's videos. Like product placement." I shrugged. "Maybe that's the way it works these days."

"Videos?"

"Here, let me show you." I searched for the video that Kai Teller had mentioned, the one of him sleeping in the New York City subway, and played it for William. After about a minute, he looked away.

"There is too much for my eyes to follow," he said, blinking.

"Yeah, quick editing is a technique. Definitely gives you a headache if you're not used to it. Sometimes, I wish I could have lived around the time you were alive."

"There is good and bad in every age, Clara."

"Yeah, I know." I thought of the Wyatts who had died of smallpox. "But when you're opening up a business and you're not the greatest techie, it's pretty bad."

"I am certain you'll do fine."

"Well, there's only so much I can do with my phone. I need to buy a laptop computer and get this place wired for internet."

"Internet?"

"It's a network that will allow me to have access to billions of computers and communicate with people all over the world."

"Is it not what your device does now?" he motioned to the phone in my hand.

"Yes, but it works on data. Whatever that is. I really don't understand it all. Just think! We'll be bringing Kensington House into the twenty-first century. Hey, we already have electricity and plumbing. There's nothing stopping us now."

One corner of William's mouth curved upward. At the very least, my enthusiasm amused him.

"Well, I'd better figure out this QR code and mailing list thing and get to bed. I have to get up at the crack of dawn to go back to Wyatt House and be there when they open the doors and Kai Teller makes his long-awaited return to society."

Bark!

"Don't worry, Boy. I haven't forgotten you."

I pulled open one of the drawers of the antique cabinet and grabbed Boy's harness. "We'll go for an extra-long walk tonight. Would you like that?"

Bark!

"Would you like to join us, William?"

"Indeed, that would be lovely."

"And you," I said to Ghost Cat, who stopped licking her paw long enough to glance at me. "You're welcome to come, too."

If Ghost Cat considered the invitation, it wasn't for long. She went right back to licking.

"That's what I figured." I laughed. "Well then, try to stay out of trouble," I said to my antisocial ghost cat and let Boy lead the way for William and me out the front door.

Chapter 5

I strode toward Wyatt House, surefooted and comfortable in my newly fixed shoe. It had been waiting for me near the front door, a short note in William's fancy cursive handwriting attached:

Dear Clara,
I hope you find the workmanship to your satisfaction.
Sincerely,
William

Like I would ever find it *less* than satisfactory. I knew William had made shoes in his lifetime, but

I certainly never expected him to fix mine. That had been so kind. He had also shined them up and gotten out all the scuff marks. That was customer service I would have been happy to tout online; unfortunately, William's business had been closed for more than a hundred fifty years, so it didn't qualify for Yelp reviews.

I had been hoping to see him and thank him personally—and also wish him happy birthday—but he wasn't around. And didn't respond to my voice. I wondered if he was tired from working on my shoe. Did ghosts even tire? Did they sleep? Questions that one day maybe I'd find the answers to.

I adjusted my purse strap, carefully balancing the coffee carrier from the Salem Beanery in my hands. No cup of coffee was going to cure the dark circles under my eyes from spending most of last night working on an online mailing list for my business, but at least I'd be alert. There was so much to learn about being an entrepreneur, and I felt like I was light-years behind everyone else. I seriously needed a computer. Working on my phone was not cutting it.

When I turned the corner, I nearly stepped on a teenager sleeping on an air mattress. When I looked closer, I realized it was the same type of mattress Kai Teller had been sleeping on and hawking the day before, the one with his face on the top cushion. As I kept walking, I saw that quite a few people were sleeping on air mattresses all along the sidewalk and in the street, which was still closed off to travel. I was pretty sure those air mattresses cost a pretty penny. That Kai Teller was a marketing genius.

"Well, here we are again," Stephanie said with a yawn as I reached the front door of Wyatt House. "Tell me why we're here again?"

"Well, we're supporting someone who is using our town as a way to make money off air mattresses." I smiled and handed her a cup of coffee. "I brought you some caffeine."

"You're a godsend." She pulled the lid off her cup and took a sip as I uncovered mine and used every ounce of strength I had not to chug it. "How are you feeling?" she asked.

"Much better, thanks. I'm thinking it was the anxiety of making the video. I know that sounds lame, but I was nervous."

"Doesn't sound lame at all," Stephanie said. "But the more you do it, the more you'll get used to it."

"Are you saying I have to do that *again*?" I asked with a laugh. I took another sip of my coffee.

"These days, you'll have to do it again and again," Stephanie said.

Great, something to look forward to.

"Good morning, all."

The guy who had been standing at the sponsor table covered with comic books walked up to us. He looked to be about forty years old and was wearing a Dave Matthews Band T-shirt; his short red hair was wet and sticking straight up as if it had been toweled dry and hair-sprayed while he was hanging upside down.

"We didn't get a chance to meet yesterday," he said to me. "I'm Vince Hughes, the owner of Ghostly Ink."

"Nice to meet you, Vince. I'm Clara."

"Owner of the Kensington House Bed-and-Breakfast," Stephanie added, nudging me with her elbow.

Ugh, I had to get used to saying that. And to carrying business cards, which I had forgotten at home where they were doing no good to anyone. "Would you like a coffee?" I asked Vince.

"That's very kind of you."

As he reached for one, I looked around for Alice, hoping I could give her the last one and get to know her a little more, but she wasn't around.

"Are those free coffees?"

Mavis was heading toward me with her hand already extended. Before I could say *back off, William slanderer* (as if I would ever say that), she plucked the last coffee from my carrier.

"Very thoughtful." Mavis opened the lid. "I usually take milk and sugar, but this will have to do." She walked back to the police barricade near the street, behind which the teens who had been sleeping outside were deflating their air mattresses and tucking them into backpacks. Beverly, not surprisingly, was standing nearby, taking photos.

"That Mavis is something else, huh?" Stephanie said.

"That's one way of putting it," I said.

"I can't believe all these people are still here." Stephanie surveyed the crowd.

"Kai's fan base is rabid," Vince said. "I think they'd follow him anywhere."

Someone was coming around the side of Wyatt House, and I realized it was Kai's assistant, Sam.

She didn't look like she had gotten much sleep. And there was something different about her. I couldn't quite put my finger on it.

"Good morning," she said with a yawn.

"Rough night?" Vince asked.

"Yeah." She ran her hands through her hair. "I don't care what Kai says," she whispered, "those air mattresses are *not* comfortable."

"Where's your baseball cap?" Vince asked.

Ah, *that's* what was missing! Sam's blue baseball cap. *Some sleuth I am.*

"That's a good question." Sam felt the top of her head absently. "I can't find it. Must be in the grass somewhere where I was sleeping."

Down the street, Alice came hurrying toward us. She was already holding a cup of coffee, so I didn't feel so bad I didn't have one for her, and she was adjusting her apron. Probably had the morning shift at The Haunted Cookie. Unless she wore that apron to sleep. Or as part of a branding strategy. *Note to self: develop a branding strategy.*

That guy Justin, who had taken the sponsor videos, arrived next, along with Kai's friends Miltos and Danny. They walked toward us from the same direction Sam had, from the side of the house. All three had slept in the grass? On Kai's mattresses? That was devotion. Justin immediately broke off from the other two and began taking videos of the crowd.

"Where's Kai's mom?" Stephanie asked.

"She's over there." Sam pointed into the assembly of fans, where Kai's mom, Linda, was chatting with some young men, including Aaron, the guy who worked at Ye Olde Salem Book Shoppe. I waved, but he didn't see me. "She slept near the front door last night—that was her post—but you would never know it by looking at her," Sam said. "She always looks so put together."

"She looks fantastic," Vince from Ghostly Ink said.

"Always," Sam said. "She's popular among Kai's fans. She tries to talk to as many people as possible at these events. She's always been so supportive of Kai."

"How many of these events does she go to?" I asked.

"Virtually all of them," Vince said, a dreamy look in his eyes. "In addition to being Kai's mom, Linda Teller is Kai's legal representative. She put herself through law school so she could provide Kai with legal services and save him some money when he was first starting out. Sometimes Kai's girlfriend, Josie, comes too. In the last episode, though, Kai said she was studying abroad in Granada, Spain."

"Wow, I couldn't have said it better myself," Sam said. "Are you a member of the Kai Krew?"

Vince nodded. "Yep. Been watching his videos since the beginning. Got my Top Fan badge on social media. I even took part in the standing challenge he did a few years ago. Didn't make it too far." He rubbed his leg. "Got a trick knee. But it was a thrill just to be there."

"Standing challenge?" I asked.

"Yeah," Miltos said when he and Danny reached us. "Kai recruited about two hundred of his fans a few years back and had them stand on spots on the floor in some old, abandoned warehouse in Nebraska. Whoever could stand the longest without sitting down won a hundred thousand dollars and the same amount went to charity." He rubbed his back. "My back hasn't been the same since."

"You're allowed to compete?" Stephanie asked.

"No, but Kai likes to have us mingle with the Krew when we can," Danny said. "The sponsors, too."

"Will the sponsors get the chance to chat with Linda?" Vince asked Sam hopefully. "I have to say, one of the reasons I wanted to sponsor this event was so I could get to chat with Kai's mom. Maybe have her sign a few comic books." His cheeks turned red, nearly matching his spiky hair.

How sweet. Kai's mom had a groupie.

"Yes, I'll be sure to let her know to stop by your table," Sam said with a smile. She looked at her watch and tapped Miltos on the shoulder. "Did you schedule the food delivery?"

"Yeah, we're all set," Miltos said. "The donut delivery from Haunted Cookie should be here in about an hour or two. Isn't that right, Alice?"

We all turned toward Alice, and she looked as if she were going to faint from the attention. She nodded meekly. "Yes." She took a sip of her coffee. I wasn't sure if she was thirsty or if she just wanted to have something in front of her face.

"How many donuts did you order?" I asked.

"About five hundred," Miltos said.

"Five hundred?" No wonder Alice had her apron on. Had she gotten any sleep last night? Maybe she had the right idea. Those hungry, restless Kai Krew members in the crowd—the ones rubbing their backs and the sleep dust out of their eyes—would probably remember the delicious donut they had from The Haunted Cookie the morning after they slept outside Wyatt House in support of their favorite YouTuber. Alice's night of no sleep would result in some international brand recognition. As opposed to *my* night of no sleep, which was only amounting to bloodshot eyes.

"All right," Sam was saying, "it's six forty-five. Let's go and—"

"Sorry, I'm late!"

Taylor Hampton was shouting from a few feet away as he made his way toward us. He looked freshly showered and appeared to be mugging for the crowd who had little interest in him.

"And you are?" Sam asked as Taylor approached the group.

"Hampton. Taylor Hampton," he said as if he were James Bond. I tried not to smirk. "I'm with the *Salem Chronicle*."

"Oh, that's right. Good morning." Sam cleared her throat and reached for the brim of the baseball cap she wasn't wearing. "As I was saying, when we go inside, if you're familiar with Kai's videos, he likes to make things a bit dramatic, so we're going to walk in, close the door, and I'm going to pretend that I'm actually afraid he didn't make it. That he had been done in by whatever ghost lives here. Just follow along. After we're all done with the theatrics, and Kai is miraculously alive, we're going to take a few photos and then you can go ahead and take down your tables. By then, the Feeding Salem people should be here, as well as the news crews, and then we're going to take a few more photos and videos. Danny, at that point, you come outside and handle things while we strike the set inside the house."

"Got it," Danny said.

"It's all about the photos and videos," Stephanie said.

"Definitely," Sam said.

"Is there any reason to do anything if you don't have a photo of it?" Danny asked. I thought he was being ironic, but he seemed serious.

Justin returned from the crowd. "Hey, man, great shirt." He pointed to Vince's Dave Matthews T-shirt.

"You like Dave Matthews?" Vince asked.

"Yeah, man. My uncle got me into them when I was a kid. He lives in Boston. We go to see them all the time."

"They did this awesome show at Burroughs Theater last weekend," Vince said. "If you've never been to a show there, they're old school. No cell phones allowed, and they use the old-fashioned tickets to get in. Dave rocked the house."

"Yeah, that was a great show."

"Um, guys." Sam looked at her watch. "Sorry to interrupt, but we're pressed for time. Justin, did you get some good stuff from the crowd?"

"Yeah. Linda was amazing. No surprise there. Some of the fans asked her to sign their air mattresses with a Sharpie."

I glanced at that Vince guy, who appeared green with envy.

"Great," Sam said. "Are we ready to shoot?"

"Ready," Justin said. "Battery is at 90 percent."

Miltos and Danny snickered.

"Justin forgot to charge his phone at the last event we did," Sam explained. "As you can imagine, Kai wasn't too happy."

"I'm sure someone else had a camera phone you could have used," I suggested.

"That's what *I* said!" Justin whined. "But Kai said he likes the way *this* phone takes photos and videos." He held his device in the air. The cover had a photo of Kai Teller being suspended in the air by a rope over what looked like Niagara Falls. "He hasn't let me upgrade in two years."

"*Anyway*," Sam said, glaring at Justin like a parent warning a child, "thank you, sponsors, so much for your support of Kai and his show. It really is for a good cause. And I hope you get lots of publicity for it." She took something plastic out of her back pocket and unfolded it. "Okay, I'll take your phones now."

"Our phones?" Stephanie asked.

"Yeah, it was in the contract you signed. I hope it's not a problem. For the stunts that aren't open to the public like this, Kai can be very protective of his space. He likes to have total control of the event. We've had issues in the past with hidden cameras and footage that's leaked before we were ready."

Stephanie definitely looked like she had a problem with handing over her phone, but after Vince and Alice put their cell phones in Sam's bag, and I did as well, she reluctantly followed along. Then Miltos and Danny slipped their phones inside the bag, too.

"You guys, also?" Stephanie asked.

"Yeah, no exceptions for us," Danny snickered. "Kai is great, but he totally has trust issues."

"Understandably so," Sam said.

"We don't really know what the next stunt is until we're there," Miltos added. "He likes to keep us on our toes."

Once the phones were all dropped in Sam's bag, she zipped it up and placed it in a small footlocker-type box outside the front door to Wyatt House. She locked the box with a key, returned the key to her pocket, and took a deep breath. "Are we ready?"

"Just waiting for Linda," Danny said.

"Linda!" Sam shouted, getting Kai's mom's attention.

"I'm assuming Linda gets to keep her phone?" Stephanie asked.

I was liking Stephanie more and more. She was forthright without appearing aggressive. She said what was on her mind, and the people around her seemed to respect her for it.

Sam nodded and shrugged. "Yeah, she keeps her phone. Not my rule."

Linda said her goodbyes to the fans, including a few hugs. I had to say, I was pretty impressed with Kai Teller's fanbase. They seemed polite and responsible. No litter in the streets. Mattresses and backpacks were already picked up and stored or carried. No drinking or roughhousing. No one trying to storm Wyatt House. Instead, they seemed to respect the police barricade as well as one another. Clearly, all those Boomers out there who had something derogatory to say about Gen Z had never met any of Kai's devoted Krew.

"I'm here. How does my hair look?" Linda ran her fingers through her dark brown hair.

"It looks great, as usual," Vince said, and his cheeks reddened again as Justin popped a lollipop into his mouth.

"A lollipop for breakfast?" Stephanie asked.

"It's cinnamon flavored," he said with a smile, as if that were a reasonable explanation.

"Your dentist must *love* you," Stephanie said.

"All right, let's do this," Sam said. She appeared to be the momma hen of the group, which seemed weird since Linda was probably double her age. Sam was the most professional among them and kept the others in line and on time. From what I could see, Kai was lucky to have her.

Sam motioned for us to walk toward the front door of Wyatt House, and as we did, members of the crowd began to clap, hoot, and holler. Miltos turned around and pumped his fist in the air, which elicited a few happy shouts. As we reached the front door, the crowd had begun to chant, "Kai! Kai!"

"Do they always do that?" I asked.

"Yep," Vince said. "It's a *Here Goes Nothing* tradition." This Vince guy seemed to know just as much—if not more—about Kai's web series as the rest of them.

"Are you ready, Justin?" Sam asked.

"Ready," he said, clicking to the camera app on his phone.

"Is this being livestreamed?" I asked.

"No, it's recorded, and then we edit this weekend for the premiere on Monday," Sam said.

Linda cleared her throat.

"Is everything okay, Linda?" Sam asked.

"Uh, yes. Good. Let's do this!" she said.

"Okay, great." Sam looked at her watch. "Go," she said to Justin.

Justin held up his phone, pressed *Record*, and Sam reached up to pull down the brim of her cap but then seemed to remember it wasn't there. She smiled broadly.

"Hey, Kai Krew! We're here in front of Wyatt House." Sam tapped on the face of her watch. "It's just before seven a.m., and we're about to open this door for the first time since leaving Kai last night. All of us—me, Justin, Miltos, Danny, and Linda, Kai's mom, slept outside the house, guarding all the windows and doors to make sure no one got in—and no ghosts got out!" She raised her voice so that she could be heard above the crowd's chanting. "So Kai has been alone—all night—in Wyatt House, which, as you heard, is considered haunted by an angry momma ghost who is looking to take revenge for the loss of her infant child. Eek! We have no idea what we'll find when we go inside." She put her hands to the sides of her face, Kevin McAllister-style. "Is Kai okay? Will he be hiding under the covers of his bed? Will he be singing lullabies with the ghost? You never know what to expect with Kai! But if he safely made it through the night, a million dollars will go to the Feeding Salem charity."

Sam nodded to Justin, and he turned the cameras on the sponsors, startling me. I was not ready for my close-up with these dark circles under my eyes, but I smiled like a dope and hoped I looked professional and didn't have a coffee mustache.

"A few of our sponsors are here with us," Sam said. "Thanks so much to Stephanie Hastings of Triple H Touring Company, Alice Sutton of The Haunted Cookie, Vince Hughes of Ghostly Ink, and Clara Kelly of the Kensington House Bed-and-Breakfast. We would have been unable to do this without you." The four of us waved awkwardly. "And a special thanks to—"

"Oh, it's my pleasure to be here!" Taylor said with a wink toward the camera.

"Um, right, this is Taylor Hampton of the *Salem Chronicle*, everyone. Local reporter extraordinaire."

Ugh, that's all Taylor needed. Another boost to his ego. He took a bow.

"What I *wanted* to say," Sam continued, "was special thanks to The Haunted Cookie and Ghostly Ink for the great swag that Kai will be handing out to the crowd later this morning. Confections and comic books! What could be better than that?!"

Linda gave Vince a kiss on the cheek on camera, surprising him, and I thought Vince might swoon. When that kiss was uploaded on Monday, something told me it would get thousands of views—from Vince watching it over and over.

"Okay, guys!" Sam said as Justin turned his lens back on her. "Are you ready to come with us?"

"Ready," Vince said, and then his cheeks flushed again. "Sorry."

"No worries! We're excited, too!" Sam looked into the camera. "Well, here goes nothing!"

Sam turned the knob of the old wooden door, which creaked open, and stepped inside. Justin let Danny, Miltos, and Linda go in front of him and waved for Taylor and the sponsors to do the same. Front-row Stephanie led the way, followed by Taylor, Vince, Alice, and me—last-row Clara (who aspired to be front-row Clara one day!). Justin followed us inside with the camera, closing the door behind him just as several news vans pulled into the street near the crowd.

It took a few moments for my eyes to adjust to the faint daylight inside Wyatt House. When they did, I glanced at my sponsor table, which, unfortunately, looked even more depressing than it had the night before.

"Hello?!" Sam called into the dark home. In front of us was Kai's air mattress, just where we had left it; Kai was under a pile of blankets, his arms holding a pillow to his face and the candles surrounding him burned down to nubs.

"Yoo-hoo!" Danny called. He tilted Justin's camera toward him and pointed to his watch. "Kai, what up?! This isn't the time to oversleep!"

Miltos grabbed Danny by the neck and jumped in front of Justin's camera. "Kai, are you there, man?" He put his hand to his ear and pretended to listen. "Hey, Mrs. T," he said to Linda, who was off-camera. "Maybe you should try waking him."

Linda stepped in front of the camera and dramatically wiped her brow. "Please, I've spent enough years trying to wake up Kai. Now, it's *your* turn."

The theatrics were fun and well-orchestrated, as if they had been rehearsed. Or maybe this was just their routine. I probably should have watched a few episodes of *Here Goes Nothing* before sponsoring this event.

Sam started tiptoeing toward the air mattress, and we all followed along like the Scooby-Doo gang. I accidentally bumped into Alice. "Sorry," I said. "I guess I should have taken a few ballet classes. My tiptoeing is rusty."

Alice glanced at me and then looked straight ahead. She didn't even crack a smile.

I thought about Beckett Miller, the first ghost I met in Salem. (Well, the *second* ghost, after William. I tended to forget sometimes that William was a ghost.) Beckett had made a comment that Alice had an anger management problem. *Very passive-aggressive. Yeah, I find that shy girls often are. Either they're meek and quiet or they want to rip your head off.* I glanced at Alice's large-rimmed glasses and checkered apron. At the hair of her ponytail swishing back and forth with every tiptoe. I didn't get an angry vibe from Alice. She came across to me like a girl who wanted to disappear.

And as a woman who, not so long ago, wanted the same thing, I was eager to find out why.

As we approached the middle of the main room, Kai was still. I couldn't imagine how he was managing to sleep with all this chatter. Part of me thought he was pretending so that Justin could keep focusing his lens on the bed and Kai could sell more air mattresses.

"Okay, Kai!" Sam said, looking at her watch and showing it to the camera. Seven a.m. on the dot. "You made it!"

Kai didn't move.

"C'mon, Kai, rise and shine!" Linda cheered.

Nothing.

Sam bent down toward Kai, and Justin brought the camera in real close.

"Boy, this guy can sleep through anything," Stephanie said with a laugh.

"Yo, Kai!" Justin kicked the air mattress. "Time to get up, man. You did it. Isn't there something you want to say to your ten-point-three million subscribers? Kai?"

"Wait, something's not right," Sam said suddenly, her face falling. "Kai's not that good of an actor." She touched his arm. "He's cold. *Really* cold. And stiff." She removed the pillow, and Kai's arms flopped away from his face; his eyes stared at the ceiling.

Wide open.

And lifeless.

He was dead.

Chapter 6

"Oh my God!" Sam screamed, falling backward.

"Whoa!" Justin said. He spread his fingers on his phone screen and zoomed in on Kai's still face. "He can't be dead."

"Justin, stop videoing! My God!" Sam said, tears flooding her eyes. "Are you crazy?"

"He's faking it, Sam. He's gotta be." Justin put the camera down. "Kai? C'mon, you fooled us, okay?" He moved closer to Kai's face and blew on it.

"Cut it out, man," Danny said, a look of shock on his face. "That's sacrilegious or something."

"Dang, he really *is* dead." Justin sat back.

We all stood there, staring at Kai's body. Hands over mouths. Eyes wide. Sobbing, in the case of Sam. Except for me. I was surprised at my indifference. What did it say about me that a dead body didn't faze me anymore?

Then we all seemed to have the same thought and turned toward Linda, who was standing as still and stiff as Kai. She stared down at him as if she couldn't believe what she was seeing—as if she *didn't* believe what she was seeing. Then, appearing to come out of a trance, she bent down and stuck two fingers by Kai's neck. She pulled her hand back. "He has no pulse. And he's ... well, Sam's right. Rigor mortis has already set in." She sat back on her legs. "He's gone."

"We need to call an ambulance," Stephanie said. She reached into her purse but then seemed to remember she didn't have her phone. "That's right. I don't have my phone."

"What the heck happened?" Vince asked. "Was it cardiac arrest?"

"I don't think so," I said.

"*I* know!" Miltos said, looking around. "It was the *ghost*. You heard what that historical society lady said. The woman who lived here was *pissed*. She wanted revenge for her dead baby."

"Let's not get carried away," Vince said.

"I'm not getting carried away," Miltos said defensively. "Maybe the ghost used its magical powers to suck the life right out of Kai!"

"Miltos," Danny said, "I don't believe in ghosts, but if I did, I don't think it works that way."

"Like *you're* the authority on ghost killings," Miltos said with a sniff.

"Could it have been an allergic reaction to something?" Vince suggested. He pointed to the snacks in the room.

"No way," Miltos said. "Every one of those snacks had been vetted by Kai. You're not going to pin this on *me*."

"I don't think it was the snacks," I said.

"Yo, Freaky Friday," Taylor said, turning to me. "I'm used to you talking to yourself, but now you're talking in riddles. You don't think it was cardiac arrest. You don't think it was an allergic reaction. What *do* you think?"

"I ..." *How do I say this?* "I ..."

Before I could finish, Linda reached out to Kai's face but then suddenly pulled her hand back. "Oh my God."

"What?" Stephanie asked.

Linda pulled off the blankets positioned at Kai's chin, revealing marks on his neck.

"What are those?" Sam asked.

"They look like choke marks," Taylor said.

"I told you!" Miltos took a few steps back. "The ghost choked the life out of Kai!" He made the sign of the cross and looked up at the ceiling.

"Kai was *killed*?" Sam asked.

"That can't be," Danny said.

Everyone was staring at Kai's body in disbelief. Except for me. Again. Instead, I was gawking at Kai's pale, gray ghost standing at the foot of the makeshift bed, watching this all play out as if on a computer screen. Which told me two things. 1) Kai hadn't died of cardiac arrest. Or an allergic reaction. If he had, his ghost would have passed on—wherever ghosts go. Foul play was definitely involved. And 2) I had somehow found myself smack dab in the middle of a murder scene.

Again.

Chapter 7

Kai's ghost glanced at me. "Hey, you, Red! Can you see me?"

Ugh. I tried to act natural. To act as interested in Kai's dead body as everyone else, but, of course, when I'm trying to act natural, that was the last thing I was. "Um, can you excuse me for a minute?" I said to the group. "I think I'm going to be sick." Yes! Vomiting was always a good reason for needing a little space. No one wanted puke on their clothing.

"I think Clara has the right idea," Stephanie said. "We should *all* get out of here."

"Good idea," Vince said when Linda stood up.

"Wait!" she said.

I didn't know what she did or said next, because Kai's ghost stood in front of me and said, "Yo, Red, you can see me, right?"

I couldn't avoid his eyes. Not with him standing right there and in my face. It would be like trying to avoid an oncoming train. But I couldn't answer him. Not without attracting attention. I nodded as imperceptibly as possible and took a couple of steps back.

"Are you nodding?" Taylor asked me.

Ugh, why was this guy always staring at me? There was a very interesting dead body in front of him to hold his attention. "Taylor, just leave me alone."

"Why are we waiting to call the police?" Stephanie asked. And I was glad she did because I missed what Linda had said the first time.

"Because if we open that door," Linda said, "and the world finds out that Kai Teller is dead and there's no other explanation for it other than being choked by an angry ghost, then those kids in Feeding Salem don't get their million dollars."

"I don't understand," Vince said.

"And I can't believe you're talking about money at a time like this," Stephanie said.

"I'm talking about hungry kids getting the funding they deserve," Linda said. "Something that was very important to Kai."

"You're taking this strangely well," Taylor said. "You realize that's your kid right there. And he was *murdered*."

"You're quite condescending, aren't you?" Linda said. "Why don't you just—"

"Red," Kai said, waving his hands in front of my face to get my attention. "I know you can see me."

I slipped my finger in front of my pursed lips in a *Shhhh* sign. Hopefully, Kai would take the hint and let me listen. By the time I focused back on the group's conversation, I totally missed Linda telling Taylor off. Darn.

"And we didn't have much when Kai was a kid, and he's made it his life's mission to help make sure kids never go hungry again," Linda was saying. "Forgive me if I'm focused right now on making sure that happens."

"She's protecting your company," I whispered to Kai.

"Well, it's too late to protect *me*. Somebody killed me!" Kai said.

"I think they already know."

Taylor kept watching me, and I covered my mouth with my hand. "So, what happened?" I whispered.

"How am *I* supposed to know what happened?" Kai asked.

Please tell me you saw the person who killed you.

Please tell me you saw the person who killed you.

Please tell me you saw the person who killed you.

If I had been wearing ruby slippers, I would have clicked the heels three times and hoped that would make my wish come true.

"I didn't see the person who killed me," Kai continued, crossing his arms. "The one time I don't have a camera on me, I'm murdered. Go figure."

Apparently, murderers were bashful nowadays and were keeping their faces hidden. "You don't remember anything about what happened?"

"No," Kai said. "I was lying down, trying to get some sleep so I could get this stupid stunt over with. It wasn't my idea to do this one."

"It wasn't?" I whispered into my hand, trying not to look at Taylor, but I could feel his eyes boring into me. "Whose idea was it?"

"My mom's. She asked if I could do something relatively safe this time. And wouldn't you know, the *one time* I don't think I'm really putting myself in danger, I get myself dead."

Wow, Kai was taking this really well. "So do you remember anything about—"

"Talking to yourself again, Freaky Friday?" Taylor asked.

I looked around. Everyone was looking at me. Great. *Say something. Stand up to this bully.*

"So, what if I am?" I said weakly. I wanted so badly to come up with a clever name for Taylor, but who was I kidding? I had named my pets Boy and Ghost Cat. I didn't have it in me. "Are you the ... the ... talking police?" *That was awful.*

"Whatever," Taylor responded.

Stephanie said, "We need to get the police here. *Now.*"

"We will," Linda said. "I just have to figure out how to open that front door without the Feeding Salem kids losing their money."

"How exactly are they losing their money?" Vince asked.

Linda let out an exasperated sigh. "Each of Kai's stunts raises money for a particular charity. And there are certain stipulations that need to be met for the money to reach its intended recipient. In this case, Kai needed to have survived in this house until seven a.m. without having been killed by a ghost."

"C'mon, Linda," Danny said. "You don't really believe that Kai was killed by a ghost, do you? You're as bad as Miltos."

"No, I don't," Linda said. "But it doesn't matter what I think. It matters what I can prove. Can I prove he *wasn't*?"

"It's common sense, isn't it?" Taylor asked.

"Maybe there *is* a medical reason Kai is deceased," Stephanie said. "But we'd need an emergency medical technician to do an exam."

"There *is* a reason," Miltos said. "Kai stopped breathing."

"Yo, Miltos, not funny," Danny said.

As Danny and Miltos began to bicker, attracting everyone's attention, I whispered to Kai, "What else do you remember?"

"I woke up and someone had their knee in my back and was choking me from behind. I couldn't see who it was."

"Is there anything else you recall?" I asked. "The feel of their hands? A smell? A sound?"

Kai thought for a moment. "No, nothing. I didn't exactly think to observe anything. And by the time I realized that … well, that I was no longer part of my body and that I was," he pointed to himself, "*this*, I was alone. Alone with my body. Stuck in this house. Shouting. Then when I heard you guys coming in, I hid upstairs."

"Why?"

"I didn't want to be here when you saw me. I don't know, I felt … embarrassed."

"Why?"

"I don't know. I guess I can't believe I let this happen to me. And then I eventually came downstairs. I tried to get my mother's attention—waving at her—but she didn't see me. No one could. But you." He looked at me. "Why can *you* see me?"

It was the question I had been asking myself for months. "I don't know. Why won't your mom let us call the police?"

"It's like you said. She's trying to protect the business. And the charity. Right now, she's thinking more like a lawyer than a mom. I'm used to it. She knows how important this business is to—"

"Are you all right?"

My eyes refocused, and I realized Linda was standing behind Kai, but as far as everyone else was concerned, she was standing in front of me.

"Yeah, I'm fine," I said. "Just feeling a bit ... light-headed."

"She does that," Taylor said. "She talks to herself."

"Better than talking to you," Stephanie said.

I smiled. I was liking Stephanie more and more.

"Listen, I know we need to call the police," Linda said. "But all I ask is that you just give me a little time. A half hour. An hour, the most. Just to figure out how we can open that door so that thousands of hungry kids don't go hungry tonight." She looked at Miltos. "Miltos!"

Miltos was near Kai's body and quickly pulled his hand away. "His body is, like, *stiff*."

"You shouldn't be touching him, Miltos," Linda was saying.

"You see?" Stephanie crossed her arms. "*This* is why we need to call the police."

"Miltos was never good at following directions," Kai told me. "He almost failed kindergarten."

"For his body to be that stiff," Vince said, "he would have had to have been dead for a while."

"How long?" Justin asked.

"I don't know," Vince said. "At least a few hours, if I were to hazard a guess."

"So, the ghost killed him sometime in the middle of the night," Miltos said.

"For the love of God," Danny said. "There's no such thing as ghosts, Miltos!"

"I guess Danny isn't too bright, either," Kai said to me.

"Let's try to keep our cool," Taylor said, suddenly taking control. "Linda asked us to give her some time to figure out how to get the charity its money. I'm familiar with Feeding Salem. It's a great organization. My brother, Clem, volunteers there. They're very underfunded. I'd like to see them get their money, too."

"We should be calling an ambulance," Stephanie huffed. "Just saying. Kai might not be dead."

"I'm dead," Kai said.

"I think he's dead," I offered.

"How do you know?" Stephanie asked.

"She doesn't," Taylor said. "Unless you got your medical license before you decided to open a bed-and-breakfast."

"Well, the sooner we can get out of here, the better," Miltos said. "Who's to say this ghost won't kill one of us next?"

"Miltos!" Danny shouted. "A ghost did not kill Kai!"

"Well, then who else could have done this?" Miltos insisted. "There was no one else in the house when we left last night. And then we each manned all the exits and windows from outside. There was no way in or out. No one was here."

"No one else that we *know of*," Stephanie said. "Someone might have been in the house before we got here and hid somewhere."

Stephanie might have been onto something. A house like this—like Kensington House—had a lot of hiding places.

"You mean, somebody may have intentionally hid in this house and planned Kai's murder?" Vince asked.

"That's *exactly* what I mean," Stephanie said. "Which is why—I hate to sound like a broken record, but—we have to call the police sooner rather than later." She looked at Alice. "What do *you* think, Alice?"

Alice? I had forgotten she was even here. She was standing off to the right, away from everyone, circling her ponytail with her finger. After a moment's pause, she said, "I think we should do whatever Kai's mom wants."

Nine words. That was the most I had ever heard come from Alice's mouth.

"Thank you," Linda said. "I appreciate that, Alice."

"I don't feel good about this," Stephanie said.

"Listen, you can do whatever you want," Linda said. "I'm not holding you hostage here. I'm just saying that if any of us opens that door and the world thinks that a ghost killed Kai, even for a moment, Feeding Salem doesn't get fed. Can *you* live with that?"

Stephanie was quiet.

"I'm asking for an hour—sixty minutes—to figure out how to fix that," Linda said.

"And how are you supposed to fix that?" Stephanie asked.

"I don't know." Linda took out her phone. "I have a digital copy of the contract we have with Feeding Salem on my phone. Maybe some of the wording in there is vague enough for me to convince a court of law that the ghost of Beth Wyatt is innocent until proven guilty. Or, at the very least, I need to convince social media. I'm not optimistic. But I can try."

"There's also another way, you know," Taylor said. "Another way of absolutely, positively knowing that your son wasn't killed by a ghost."

"And what's that?" Linda asked.

"We figure out who killed Kai ourselves."

Chapter 8

"You've got to be kidding," Stephanie said. "We're not detectives. Show of hands: Everyone in here with vast experience tracking down murderers, raise your hand."

I put my hands behind my back. I didn't have *that* much experience. Certainly not *vast*. I had only done it twice.

"See?" Stephanie continued. "The best thing to do is—"

Creak...

"What was that?" Sam asked as we all looked up.

"I don't know, but it came from there." Vince pointed to the ceiling.

"It's the ghost!" Miltos exclaimed.

I thought of my first morning in Kensington House. That same creak. William. Could there really be a ghost upstairs or was that just the house settling, as they say? I was probably the only one in the room who knew a ghost was a real possibility. And maybe Kai.

"Okay, even *I'm* getting a little freaked out now," Stephanie said. "And I run a hauntings tour through Salem."

"I'm with the tour lady," Miltos said. "We should get out of here."

"It's no ghost, Miltos," Danny said. "But …"

"But what?" I asked.

"What if it's the person who killed Kai?" Danny asked. "What if Stephanie was right? What if they're still hiding in the house?"

We all looked at each other.

"I say again," Stephanie said. "Then we should call the cops."

"I agree," I said. No more sleuthing for me.

"If we wait, we risk the person getting away," Taylor said.

"How? There's a ton of people outside," Vince said.

"There were a ton of people outside last night, too. And the killer could have managed to get in."

"Aren't there tunnels under Salem?" Linda said.

"Some, yes," Vince said.

And trapdoors, too, I wanted to add.

"You think he came in through a tunnel?" Danny asked.

It seemed possible. Before I could offer my two cents, Danny and Taylor looked at one another and charged upstairs, with Justin following, holding his camera in front of him. Kai left my side and began running after them.

"You shouldn't go up there!" Stephanie was yelling fruitlessly.

Heavy footsteps pounded the ceiling, running from one side of Wyatt House to the other, causing dust to trickle down. Then, suddenly, it was quiet.

"Oh no!" Miltos said. "The ghost got them."

"Really, Miltos?" Sam shook her head.

"Do we have to go through all this?" Stephanie asked Linda. "Can't you just give the charity the money afterward? So what if it doesn't come directly from the money raised from this event?"

"No, I can't," Linda said. "For two reasons. One, the money is earmarked for Feeding Salem and was raised by Kai *specifically* for this particular stunt. And the language of the donation contract states that if Kai doesn't walk out that door and the world thinks he was killed by a ghost, the money goes back to the donors. And, two, do you think I have a million dollars lying around?" Linda appeared incredulous. "Pretty much everything Kai raises goes to charity. We have enough of a profile with *Here Goes Nothing* to have a roof over our heads in a middle-class neighborhood and maybe save a little for retirement." She held up her phone. "Unfortunately, though, I'm looking at this contract, and I'm not coming up with anything."

"I can take a look at it, Linda, if you'd like," Vince said. "I was pre-law before I opened the comic book store."

"Really?" she asked. "What made you change?"

"I wanted to move from the villains to the superheroes." He shrugged. "I'd be happy to help."

Linda handed him the phone. "Great, see what you think."

For a moment, I thought Vince might use Linda's phone to call the police, but I could see he still had that gaga look on his face when it came to Linda Teller. He wouldn't do anything to upset her. And he would probably scour that contract until his eyes were bloodshot so that he could have the chance of being her personal superhero.

More running upstairs.

Miltos breathed a sigh of relief. "They're alive, at least," he said.

"Yeah, but this is a crime scene," Stephanie said, "and they're totally disrupting it up there. Taylor Hampton, as a journalist, should *know* that."

"Their DNA and hair fibers were up there anyway," Sam offered. "We were all over this house yesterday."

"Yeah, but Taylor wasn't upstairs," Stephanie said. "And if Taylor killed Kai, and his hair fibers or DNA or whatever are upstairs, now there's a reason for it *other* than murder."

"You seriously think that newspaper guy killed Kai?" Sam asked.

Stephanie shrugged. "Anything is possible."

She was right, but I doubted it. As gross as Taylor Hampton was, I couldn't really see him getting his hands dirty.

Suddenly, Taylor, followed by Danny and Justin, appeared at the top of the stairs.

"Well?" Linda asked as they slowly made their way down.

"Did you see the ghost?" Miltos asked.

"There's no ghost, Miltos," Danny said when he got to the bottom. "Get over yourself."

"But we *did* find something," Justin said.

"What?" Linda asked.

Taylor took two steps forward with his hand behind his back. And then, in a dramatic fashion, as if he were a magician making a bouquet of flowers materialize out of thin air, he showed us his hand.

In it, was Sam's blue baseball cap.

Chapter 9

"Where did you find that?" Sam asked, reaching for it, but Taylor pulled it away.

"Upstairs," he said. "Behind one of the radiators. Near one of the windows at the side of the house."

"Near where *you* were supposed to be stationed outside," Danny said.

"So?" Sam said. "Why are you looking at me like that, Danny?"

"Why do you *think*?" Danny asked.

"Sam, you killed Kai?" Miltos asked.

"What? You can't be serious," Sam said.

"*Sam* killed me?" Kai suddenly appeared next to me. "She's been with me since the beginning.

When I just had the idea for the show. She was always so supportive. Why would she do it?"

I couldn't answer Kai, not without drawing attention to myself. But I was just as surprised. Sam appeared to be the only one who had a strong emotional reaction when seeing Kai's dead body. Even Linda seemed a bit detached and composed.

"I mean, really?" Sam said. "Why would I kill Kai?"

"Who knows?" Danny said. "He *could* be annoying sometimes."

"Annoying?" Kai said.

"Danny," Sam said, "if I killed everyone who annoyed me, I would have done away with *you* a long time ago."

"Nice one," Justin said, holding the camera up.

"Justin, put the damn camera down!" Sam said.

"Kai said to always keep the camera running," Justin said. "You never know when you're going to get good stuff. I'm honoring his memory."

"Whatever." Sam rolled her eyes. "When, exactly, was I supposed to have done this?"

"Sometime in the middle of the night, maybe," Miltos said.

"I wasn't asking *you*, Miltos."

"You *were* the last one out last night," Danny noted.

"Yeah, and I was with *her*." Sam pointed to me. "I was waiting for her to get out of the bathroom so we could tiptoe out and not bother Kai, who was alive, by the way, when we left. Right, Clara?"

I didn't know what to say. I assumed Kai was alive (why wouldn't he be?), but I couldn't be sure.

"I remember you leaving," Kai said. "I heard you and Sam whispering. I remember because I was annoyed that you were still here and I wanted to get to sleep, and you weren't listening to directions." He shrugged. "Sorry."

"I'm pretty sure he was alive," I offered to the group.

"And I was wearing my blue baseball cap, if you all remember," Sam said.

"That's right. She was," Miltos said. "Good point."

"None of that means anything," Taylor said.

"What are you talking about?" Sam said. "It means *everything*."

"You could have very easily slipped into the house after everyone was gone, killed your friend, and lost your hat sometime after that before leaving the house again," Taylor said as if he were hosting a true crime documentary.

Justin zoomed the camera onto Sam's face.

"Justin ..." Sam balled her hand into a fist. "If you don't take that camera out of my—"

"I was wondering where your baseball cap was all morning," Danny said.

"I had it on when I went to sleep," Sam said.

"But not when you woke up," Danny noted.

"Exactly."

"Exactly."

"Danny! Seriously?!" Sam's cheeks were red now, and her voice agitated. "Are we really turning on each other? We've been friends forever."

"Okay, people, broken record here," Stephanie said, "but you *do* realize that if Kai's DNA is on that cap, you're totally messing with it. If you really care about what happened to your friend Kai, then you know what I think you should do."

Sam wasn't listening. "Do you think I'm stupid, Danny? If I killed Kai and left my cap here, don't you think I would come looking for it?"

"Maybe you couldn't," Miltos said. "Maybe it would risk someone seeing you."

"Maybe that's also why you looked so awful this morning," Justin said. "Like you hadn't slept at all."

"I look so awful because I slept on one of Kai's uncomfortable air mattresses last night," Sam said.

"Did she say *uncomfortable*?" Kai asked me.

"Maybe you look awful because of the guilt of what you did," Linda said to Sam, who practically gasped at the insinuation.

"Yeah, the only one who looks like they got even less sleep than you is *her*." Danny pointed to me. *Great.*

"Linda," Sam pleaded. "You *know* that—"

"I don't know anything. I know my son is dead and your baseball cap mysteriously disappeared sometime last night and somehow ended up on the second floor of a building that you weren't supposed to be in."

"Please," Sam pleaded, "I couldn't have killed Kai. I ... I ..."

"Admit it?" Miltos asked.

"No, *idiot*." Sam struggled with the words. "I ... I loved Kai."

"You *loved* him?" Danny asked.

"She *loved* me?" Kai echoed.

"Yes, I loved him." Sam exhaled fiercely, like she was releasing a long-held breath. "I've loved him ... forever. I never said anything. He kinda just saw me as one of the guys. I guess I was hoping that would change one day. Why do you think I took this crappy job? I was pre-med before this."

"Okay, that's pathetic," Danny said.

"You're pathetic, Danny," Sam said.

"He's dating someone, Sam," Danny said. "You know that."

"Not anymore," Kai told me. "I broke up with her yesterday over text."

My hand flew to my mouth. "Did Sam know?" I whispered, adding, "Over text? Really?"

Kai shook his head. "I don't think Sam knew. I didn't tell anyone yet."

"Because he's dating someone is why I didn't say anything," Sam was saying.

"I can't believe she loved me," Kai said again.

"Maybe you were jealous," Danny said to Sam.

"Don't be a jerk, Dan. Can't you see? Someone is trying to frame me," Sam said.

I pulled my pendant out from under my shirt and rubbed it. I believed Sam. That was what my gut was telling me. She seemed to care about Kai. *And* his company. But if it wasn't Sam, then who killed Kai Teller? And why?

"Kai! Kai! Kai!" More chanting outside. Much louder than before.

"They're getting antsy out there," Taylor said.

"How do we tell them that Kai is dead?" Danny asked.

"Maybe we don't have to," Miltos suggested.

"Um, don't you think they'll be suspicious when the front door of Wyatt House opens and Kai's not there?" Danny asked.

"Maybe Miltos has a point," Sam said. "They're going to figure it out on their own when the haunted house episode doesn't run on Monday."

"It wasn't running anyway," Linda said.

"What do you mean?" Sam asked.

Linda shrugged. "It was supposed to be a surprise."

"What kind of surprise?" I asked.

"I'm not supposed to say," Linda said.

"Seriously? At this point?" Stephanie asked.

"We were pushing the haunted house episode to the following week."

"Why?" Sam asked.

"Well, in its place, we were running a special episode. Kai was calling it the 'Where Do I Come From?' episode."

"I changed the name," Kai whispered to me.

"'Where Do I Come From?'" Sam asked. "What is it about?"

Linda hesitated. Strangely, she looked more uncomfortable now than she did when she discovered that her son had been murdered. "Well, Kai ... well, he thought it might be fun to learn all about the people who make the *Here Goes Nothing* web show happen."

"Without talking to any of us?" Sam asked.

"Well, it wasn't that kind of show."

"What kind of show was it?" Miltos asked.

"Well, Kai …" Linda took a deep breath. "All right, he pulled DNA from all of you and did a genealogy search."

"He did *what*?" Sam asked. "Without asking for our permission?"

"Typical Kai," Justin said, holding the camera up toward Linda's face.

"Is that why he had me spit in a tube that time?" Miltos's eyebrows raised.

"He told me it was saliva testing for biomarkers," Danny said. "You know, for insurance premiums or something. To detect cancer or periodontal disease."

"I am *such* a good liar." Kai winked at me.

"He just thought it would be fun. That's all," Linda said.

"Fun?" Stephanie asked, furrowing her brows.

"You're always defending him, Linda," Danny said.

"That's my job," Linda said. "I'm his mom."

"Why didn't I know about this?" Sam asked. "I was his personal assistant."

"Nobody knew," Linda said. "What does it matter now anyway? No one is going to see it."

"Why not?" Stephanie asked.

"Kai did this on his own. The research. The editing. I have no idea where he's keeping that episode. In some folder with some password I don't know. He kept it separate from the rest of the show stuff. He was so paranoid one of you would find out. Now that episode will be lost forever."

"The password is *MiltosIsAnIdi0t!*," Kai said to me. "Initial caps. A zero instead of an O in *idiot*, and an exclamation point at the end. Tell my mother, okay? There's no reason that episode has to die just because I did."

"We're better off without that episode," Miltos said. "Who knows what a genealogy search would turn up. If I know Kai, he probably found some juicy stuff."

"Kai! Kai! Kai!" The cheering from the front of the house continued.

"We can't wait any longer," Sam said. "Even if you think *I* did this. We should call the cops and have them do a *real* investigation."

"Finally, a voice of reason," Stephanie said.

I glanced at Vince, who was staring at Linda's phone, his eyes wide.

"What is it, Vince?" I asked.

"Did you find anything?" Linda asked.

"Um," Vince said, his cheeks turning red and matching his hair again. "I did, but ..."

"Well, what is it?" Danny asked.

"Um ..." Vince glanced at Linda, who shrugged.

"What?" she said. "What did you find?"

"Well …" He held up the screen. "Linda's right. It says that if Kai loses his life during this stunt, and the cause of death is undetermined by seven a.m. this morning, as documented by video," he glanced at Justin, "the charity of choice doesn't receive its funds and the donations are returned to the donors."

"I told you," Linda said.

"But there's more," Vince said, looking at Linda with puppy-dog eyes.

"So?" Linda said. "Out with it."

Vince took a breath. "It also says that if Kai was to lose his life during this stunt, or in any of his stunts, the business—and all its intellectual property—is bequeathed to *you*, Linda."

"Yeah?" Linda crossed her arms. "So? I'm his mother."

"Yeah." Taylor smiled smugly. "And now you're also a murder suspect."

Chapter 10

"Okay, now you're getting ridiculous," Linda said.

"Are we?" Taylor brought his hand to his temple as if he were Columbo. "Where exactly *were* you last night, Linda?"

"I refuse to answer that question."

"I kinda think you have to, Linda," Danny said.

Linda exhaled loudly. "Where do you *think* I was? I was shmoozing with Kai's Krew until about ten or eleven p.m., and then I was sleeping in front of the house where hundreds of people saw me."

"You were there all night?" I asked.

Everyone looked at me, and that's when I realized the words had come out of my mouth. Oh no. Was I sleuthing?

"You think my *mother* killed me?" Kai asked.

I tried to shrug imperceptibly so that no one would notice, but no one was looking at me anyway. Everyone was waiting to hear Linda's answer to my question.

"Yes, I was there, in front of the house, all night." Linda said. "Except ..."

"Aha!" Miltos said.

"Give it a rest, Miltos," Linda said. "I was going to say, except to go to the bathroom."

But Miltos was right. In addition to having a motive—although I agreed with Linda that it was weak—she also had opportunity.

"And where did you go to the bathroom?" Taylor asked.

"Where do you think? In the porta-potty behind this creepy old house, where everyone was told to go."

"How long were you gone from your post?" Sam asked.

"You too?" Linda said. "You think I killed my own son?"

"It doesn't feel so great, Linda, to be accused of hurting someone you love, does it?"

Linda shook her head. "I don't know ... I was gone, maybe, fifteen minutes."

"Fifteen minutes to pee?" Taylor said.

"Very suspicious," Miltos said. "Most mammals—humans included—urinate in about twenty seconds. And that's regardless of their size."

"I don't need a science lesson, Miltos." Linda rolled her eyes.

"Yeah, but you might need a lawyer," Taylor said.

"Listen to yourselves!" Linda said. "You're not thinking clearly. Who else is Kai supposed to leave everything to? *You*, Danny? Who just called him annoying? *You*, Miltos? You would forget your own head if it wasn't attached to your body. For all Kai's life, it's been just me and him. The two of us. We're all we had. Each other. If something happened to me, Kai would have gotten everything I have. And, of course, vice versa. You're all letting your imaginations run wild. And have seen too many cop shows."

"Maybe so, but there's been one person telling us that we can't go to the police, and it's the one person who has a motive," Stephanie said.

"What about Sam?" Linda pointed her finger. "You found her baseball cap upstairs."

"Okay, so now you're throwing *me* under the bus?" Sam asked. "Maybe you put it there."

"That's it. I'm leaving," Stephanie said.

"Open that door, and I'll sue you!" Linda said with an intensity that startled me. And I wasn't the only one. The room got very quiet.

Stephanie crossed her arms. "I thought you weren't holding me hostage?"

"I'm not, but ..." Linda looked up at the ceiling and took a deep breath. "I just—"

"Holy cow!" Vince said. "You have to see this." Still holding Linda's phone, he held it up, and we all gathered around it. The screen was dark, and I had to squint to try to make out what was happening.

"What are we looking at?" Danny asked.

"It's camera footage from one of Kai's fans who spent the night in front of Wyatt House," Vince said. "He videoed himself talking to the camera. But look ..." He pointed to the front of the house, where Linda was arranging the blankets on her air mattress.

"I told you I was there," Linda said with satisfaction.

Then Vince pointed away from Linda and to the side of Wyatt House.

"What is *that*?" Stephanie asked, moving closer to the screen.

"Is that a person?" Miltos asked.

"Yes, I think so," Vince said. "It looks like someone is climbing up the trellis. It looks like they're trying to get to the second-floor window."

"Clearly, that's not me," Linda said with a look of vindication, although someone scaling the exterior of Wyatt House didn't exactly exonerate her just yet. The two could have been working together. *Why am I thinking like a detective?*

"It looks like that person is climbing up to the same window where we found Sam's baseball cap," Justin said.

Vince took a screenshot of the video and zoomed into it, but it was too dark and pixelated to identify the wannabe Spider-Man. The only thing we could see for sure was that whoever it was had on a dark-colored baseball cap. That, or we were looking at the bill of a human-sized duck sneaking into Wyatt House.

"A baseball cap," Danny said.

"That is *not* me, Danny," Sam said.

"Sam, it's not looking good," Linda said.

"Does it say anything in the video's comments?" Justin asked.

"I looked them over. People are speculating about what's going on, but no one has made any kind of positive ID," Vince said.

"But the Kai Krew knows something's up?" Danny said.

"Hard to say," Vince said. "They know someone is scaling the wall, but they don't know who it is or what it means. For all they know, it's a handyman or an electrician or whatever. They certainly don't know Kai is dead."

"They will soon," Taylor said.

"Wait, look," I said as Vince zoomed out of the image. "There's something there at the bottom right."

Vince zoomed in on the bottom right of the photo, making it even more pixelated, but it was pretty clear that there was a leg. Two legs, actually. And they looked like they were lying on an air mattress.

"See?" Sam said. "That's me. I'm sleeping there. Someone took my cap and put it on their head to make it look like I was going into the house."

"How do we know that's *you* on the air mattress?" Taylor asked.

"Who else would it be?" Sam asked.

"I don't know. Maybe you're working with someone," Miltos said, "and you had them lie down on the mattress while you went inside and killed Kai." He seemed excited that he had put that together himself.

"That's insane, and you know it, Miltos," Sam said.

"Right now, *everything* is insane," Stephanie said.

The bickering and finger-pointing continued. I looked over to the side of the room where Alice was by herself, appearing horrified by what was taking place. I realized at that moment that Alice and I had something in common. We were the only ones here who had found themselves associated with at least three (at present count, anyway) homicides. Beckett Miller's. Marlena Ryder's. And now Kai Teller's. Talk about a weird club to belong to. I'd heard people say politics made strange bedfellows. Apparently, so did murder.

Kai was still standing beside me, looking at his family and friends with interest. Or maybe confusion. Possibly sadness. It was one thing to find out someone had taken away your life. It was quite another to realize it might have been someone you knew and trusted.

I was about to step in and tell everyone to take a breath when a loud *creak* came from somewhere upstairs. We all looked up at the ceiling.

"There it is again," Danny said. "That noise."

"It's the ghost of Beth Wyatt!" Miltos said. "She's getting ready to kill again!"

"Geez!" Danny shouted. "For the love of—"

"I don't know about that, Miltos," Justin said calmly. "But if that video proves that someone was trying to get in the house, then that person really might still be here."

"But you checked already," I said.

"We stopped looking when we found Sam's baseball cap," Danny explained. "There's more of the house to explore."

"Yeah, and not only that, but by now, maybe the killer—if there *is* one up there—moved spots." Justin turned his camera lens around so that it was facing him. "We'd have to recheck the entire floor before the killer disappears—maybe into the underground tunnels," he said to his phone screen.

"Enough with the video, Justin," Danny said.

"Kai would have wanted me to!" Justin whined.

"Kai's not here anymore," Linda said, and for the first time, I detected a hint of sadness in her voice. Maybe the shock of what happened was finally wearing off and the next stage of her grief was beginning.

"Kai never wanted you on camera anyway, Justin," Miltos said.

"Yeah," Danny said, "he liked to say that some faces were made for the big screen and others were made for—"

"Behind the scenes," Kai said with him.

"You guys are wrong," Justin said. "He was going to give me my chance. He told me so."

"I was *never* going to let Justin have a big role on camera," Kai said to me. "I just told him that so he would stop asking me."

Well, *that* was gross. Kai had been leading Justin on, making him think he wanted what was best for him when he never planned on giving Justin the support he needed. Ick. Kai was reminding me of Joe, pretending to be my faithful and devoted husband when, really, he was a narcissist and liar. I much preferred the real-awful Joe over the pretend-luvie Joe. At least I knew what I was up against. I glanced toward the front door and wondered how the Kai Krew would feel about finding out their fearless leader was a manipulative jerk.

"Enough of this. We're running out of time," Taylor said. "I'll go upstairs and check out the noise." He pushed out his chest as if it had a big S on it.

"There are too many rooms to cover for one person," Danny said. "We should all go."

"I'm not going anywhere," Linda said. "I'm staying with Kai."

"Then I'll stay, too," Stephanie said.

"You don't need to," Linda said.

"Maybe I do." Stephanie raised her eyebrows.

"What are you implying?" Linda put her hands on her hips.

"I'm implying that your son has been killed, and we don't know what's happened. Nobody should be left alone."

"She's right," Sam said. "Stephanie, you stay here with Linda. And Alice, too. We'll check this house one last time. Thoroughly. And in pairs. And then, after we've made sure that no one else is in the house, we'll call the police. Agreed?"

Everyone nodded their heads, but Sam was looking at Linda. "Right, Linda?" she asked.

Linda nodded. "All right."

"Thank God," Stephanie said.

"All right." Sam reached for the baseball cap on her head again, forgetting it wasn't there. "Vince, come with me. Danny, you go with Taylor. Miltos, you go with Clara."

"Me? I'm not going up there!" Miltos exclaimed. "You guys are nuts. There's a ghost up there who killed Kai, and you want us to go walking up there without any weapons!"

"Trust me, Miltos," Danny said. "The world is a safer place without there being a weapon in your hands."

"Yeah, don't worry, Miltos," Justin said, motioning to me. "This nice woman will protect you." He focused his camera lens on Miltos and then on me. "What about me, Sam? Who do *I* go with?"

"Keep filming. You were right about Kai. He would have wanted you to keep filming. Pick a group and stick with them. But no one is to be alone."

I didn't know what had gotten into Sam, but she seemed to be back to her old self. Taking control.

In command. I remembered what she said about being pre-med in college and suddenly pictured her performing a complicated surgery. Or running a movie studio. Or a marathon. Sam gave me the impression that she could be anything she wanted to be but had chosen to stick with Kai Teller ... *out of love?* If there were some kind of list of women who did stupid things, I would be at the top (marrying Joe, duh) and Sam could arguably take second place. From what I'd seen, Kai should have been working for *her*.

"Kai! Kai! Kai!" There was a renewed chanting outside, this time with a chorus of young children.

"The Feeding Salem people must be here," Linda said.

"We don't have much time," Vince said.

Suddenly, the chorus of "Who Let the Dogs Out" filled the room. Linda reached for her phone. "I don't recognize the number," she said. "What should I do?"

"Let it go to voicemail for now," Sam said. "You can always say you were away from your phone."

Linda nodded as our little Scooby-Doo group of amateur sleuths walked toward the staircase.

"We gotta open that door soon," Vince said with gravity. "I don't think the Krew is going to wait much longer."

I agreed, imagining a band of angry Krew members with pitchforks storming Wyatt House and stumbling upon the dead body of their leader. I wasn't sure we were going to find anything upstairs, but I suddenly wanted to be as far away from the front door as possible.

Chapter 11

Danny and Taylor led the way, followed by Justin, who held the camera in front of him. Next was Sam and Vince. Miltos and I—and Kai, too—brought up the rear, although Miltos was about two steps behind me. "Isn't there another way?" he pleaded.

"No, Miltos," Danny said, walking up the stairs. "Pull up your big-boy pants, and stop whining."

"Guys!" Linda called, her phone to her ear. "I got a voicemail. The call was from the Feeding Salem people letting me know they brought several families they work with this morning, the families designated to be the recipients of Kai's donation. They said they're excited to see Kai." She looked down at Kai's dead body. Kai wasn't going to walk out of Wyatt House to greet the Feeding Salem families or his fans. He was never going to walk anywhere again. Stephanie put her hand on Linda's shoulder. Danny gave Linda a thumbs-up and continued walking with Taylor.

Miltos reached up and pulled the hair tie out of his manbun, letting his long, dark locks loose around his face. "I'm ready," he said. Maybe he figured that if the biblical Samson could draw his strength from his hair, then he needed as much hair accessible to him as possible.

The higher we climbed, the colder it got. Miltos rubbed his arms. "Why is it so chilly up here? I thought warm air rises."

"It's probably the cold air from outside getting in," Taylor said. "This old house has lots of problems, which is why the historical society is renovating it. A storm last year caused part of the room at the back of the house to cave in, and they threw up some roofing cement to hold the shingles in place—until they could get a roofer to take care of the damage properly. Which they never did."

"How do you know so much about this house?" Vince asked.

"I did a story on it for the *Chronicle* a few months back," Taylor said.

"This is a stupid idea," Miltos muttered. So far, the loose hair was doing nothing to boost his confidence.

"Yo, Miltos, you're such a baby," Kai said. He was walking up the stairs next to me, trying to hold on to the railing, but his hand kept slipping through the wood. I wanted to tell him that fine motor skills were something a ghost would develop over time, but I couldn't without looking ... well, *freaky*, as Taylor might say.

"Do you believe in ghosts?" Miltos asked me suddenly.

What to say? I glanced at Kai's ghost next to me. Clearly, I did believe in ghosts, and while my new motto in life was to tell the truth (as much as possible), I didn't think this was the right time. "Let's just concentrate on finding out what's going on," I said tactfully.

"What's going on is a bitter ghost took out her frustrations on my friend Kai," Miltos said. "And now we're looking for her so that she can do the same to us."

"Miltos, enough already," Sam said.

"He's not necessarily wrong, you know," Kai said to me.

"What?" I said before I could stop myself.

"Oh, please, don't start talking to yourself," Miltos said.

"I'm not talking to *myself.*" *Hooray for the truth!*

"That doesn't make me feel better," Miltos said.

"What I mean is, I didn't see who did this to me," Kai said to me. "It *could* have been the ghost." He shrugged his gray shoulders.

Yeah, I guess it could have been. But, so far, the ghosts I had been acquainted with hadn't been killers. They could be thieves and not the nicest people, but murderers? And I refused to believe William, alive or dead, would harm anyone unless provoked. William was thoughtful and kind, despite what the history textbooks said. One of the best people I had ever known. If Beth Wyatt was, indeed, roaming the halls of Wyatt House somewhere, odds were she wasn't the one who killed Kai. I'd bet my life on it. (But I hoped I didn't have to.)

As we reached the second floor, the stairwell led into a central hallway with what looked like identical rooms on each side of the house. Taylor was right. Near the back, toward the ceiling, was water damage marked by peeling wallpaper and a sloppy repair job. The historical society's renovation couldn't come soon enough, but lucky for us, whatever cracks were in the home's exterior—and there were quite a few—let in enough daylight for us to see.

When we all reached the top of the staircase, Taylor took charge. "Danny and I will take those two bedrooms," he said, pointing to the front-left side of the house. "Sam, you and Vince check out those back two rooms. And Miltos, you and Clara circle around and take the two rooms on the front right. If there's someone in this house, we'll find him. Or her."

"Shouldn't someone stand guard at the top of the steps?" Miltos offered. "This way, no one can sneak down the stairs while we're all occupied in the other rooms." He raised his hand. "I volunteer!"

Taylor shook his head. "Not necessary. The others are at the bottom of the stairs and will see someone if they go down."

"Nice try, though, Miltos," Danny said with a smirk. "You can hold that nice woman's hand, though, if you need to."

"Shut up, Danny," Miltos said.

"Guys, focus," Taylor said. "When you're done with your search, wait for the others here, and we'll regroup and exchange notes. Everyone agreed?"

As much as I didn't like being told what to do by Taylor Hampton, it seemed like a reasonable plan. Everyone nodded their heads.

"C'mon, Miltos," I said. "It'll be okay."

"That's easy for *you* to say." Miltos rubbed his arms. "Is it possible to get frostbite indoors?"

"Yes, maybe in the Arctic, Miltos," Sam said.

"Dude, it's like sixty degrees outside," Kai said, shaking his head. I was pretty sure Kai had no idea that *he* was the one giving Miltos the chills.

We spread out, with Miltos and me heading toward the front two rooms on the right-hand side. I knew I was supposed to be looking for a murderer, but it was hard not to admire the workmanship of the home. Yes, Wyatt House was in dire need of repairs and renovation, but it had that same colonial quaintness that Kensington House and other homes in the area had. There was a steeply pitched roof and a central chimney that was massive and oblong. The few windows on this floor were small, diagonal-shaped, and somewhat asymmetrical. And although the walls were mostly bare, with minimal decoration, it was clear to me that John Wyatt had built this place with love and tenderness as much as wood and nails.

We got to the first room, which was roped off.

"I don't think we're supposed to go in here," Miltos said, probably already looking for an excuse to go back downstairs. "We can get in trouble."

I had a feeling we were in trouble already and pretty sure the Salem Historical Society wasn't going to be too happy to find out someone had been murdered in one of their homes and that a ghost was the primary suspect. On the flip side, when word got out, even more people might be coming to Salem this Halloween. People seemed to love the macabre.

"Just don't touch anything," I said, "and we'll be okay."

There was another one of the Salem Historical Society's large laminated signs atop an easel near the entrance to the room.

Primary Bedroom

This room served as the primary bedroom of John and Beth Wyatt. Although she once aspired to be a dancer on stage, Beth took to homemaking, sewing all her linens and curtains and taking great pride in her handiwork. Upon Beth's death, John Wyatt decided to leave the room as it was and slept mostly in the spare room across the hall, next to the nursery. The furnishings are as they were then.

I hesitated before stepping over the velvet rope. I was used to following directions and doing what I was told—I imagined a series of alarms sounding or a giant Indiana Jones-esque boulder rolling on top of me the minute I placed my foot across the threshold. But it was possible that someone was hiding in there—a someone who killed Kai Teller—and I was pretty sure there was no way Miltos was going in first, so I had to just do it.

"Yo, if no one is going to go in, then I'll go," Kai said, stepping over the velvet rope.

I wanted so badly to tell Kai that he could walk through walls and didn't have to deal with velvet ropes or doorknobs, but with Miltos here, I couldn't risk the conversation.

"Aren't you going to go first?" Miltos asked me, fear in his eyes—well, as much of his eyes as I could see behind his long strands of hair.

"Sure," I said as if there was nothing to be afraid of. He may have feared the wrath of Beth Wyatt, but I was more concerned about the wrath of Mavis from the Salem Historical Society. I stepped over the rope anyway and found myself inside the Wyatts' master bedroom.

"This place is a dump," Kai said, looking around.

I totally disagreed. Sure, the room was drab and dusty, but there was much to admire. The high ceiling had an open-beam construction, and the striped wallpaper adorning the walls—although faded—was cheerful. Two portraits—of a man and a woman—looked like larger versions of a broach that might be worn on a woman's lapel. Was that John and Beth Wyatt? In the corner of the room was an upholstered chair, a throw blanket draped over one of the arms, and a pair of knitting needles on its cushion. It wasn't hard to imagine Beth Wyatt sitting there, gazing out the window while she sewed.

"Is this the room where they found Sam's hat?" Miltos asked, peeking his head in.

"No," I said. "I think it was the other room. The one next to this one. We'll go there next."

"Yay, something to look forward to," Miltos said with sarcasm.

There was a narrow door at the far end of the room, which, I assumed, led to a closet, but then I thought of the secret rooms in Kensington House. Could that narrow door lead to a secret room? But for what purpose? And, more importantly, could the murderer be hiding in there?

Ugh. I was supposed to be the one answering that last question. That was why I was here. I summoned my courage and reached for the knob.

"What are you doing?!" Miltos said. "You said not to touch anything."

"Yeah, but we're supposed to check the rooms. I need to open the door."

"But what if the murderer is hiding in there? Are you just going to stand there while he kills you?"

He had a point. I looked around, placed my purse on the floor, and reached for one of the knitting needles.

"You're not supposed to touch those, either!" he shrieked.

"Dude!" Kai said.

Before Miltos could say anything else or I lost my nerve (whichever came first), I held the knitting needle in front of me like a sword and yanked the narrow door open as Miltos hid his eyes behind his hands—and hair. But there was nothing behind the door other than a stack of boxes on which someone had scribbled *Property of the Salem Historical Society*.

"Are we dead?" Miltos asked.

"Not yet," Kai said and then turned to me. "If I could figure out how to get my hand around one of those knitting needles, Miltos might be, though."

I pulled one of the boxes down, thinking it might be a clue of some kind, but when I unflapped the lid, I saw there were just stacks of paperwork inside.

"Yo, do you know how many trees died to make this?" Kai asked, pointing to the box with a shake of his gray head. "And it's just sitting in here, discarded. Last year, we raised half a million dollars for a reforestation project because of stuff like this. I had to spend the night in a tree getting eaten by mosquitoes because people don't recycle."

"Sounds fun," I said.

"What sounds fun?" Miltos asked.

I shook my head. "Nothing." I returned the box to the closet and the knitting needle to the upholstered chair, placing it back the way it was.

"Well, there's no one here," Miltos said with relief and a glimmer of hope. "I guess we can go back downstairs."

"We still need to check the other room," I said. "Remember, that's the one where the person who was climbing the trellis was trying to go, the one where they found Sam's baseball cap."

"Did you have to remind me?" he asked.

I hopped back over the velvet rope and turned left toward the front of Wyatt House. One of those asymmetrical windows was in front of me, and I crouched down to avoid it, not wanting to attract anyone's attention on the outside. Kai did the same.

"You don't need to do that," I told him.

"Do what?" Miltos asked.

"Oh," Kai said, "that's right." He began jumping up and down in front of the window and shouting, "Yo! Look at me! I'm a ghost!"

I immediately regretted what I said. There was a definite chance—with all those hundreds of pairs of eyes out there—that *one* of them would be able to see Kai. Luckily, Kai got bored quickly and entered the front room, bypassing another one of the historical society's laminated signs, which was stationed outside the doorway.

Spare Bedroom

Beth and John Wyatt intended this small-sized room to be a nursery for their firstborn child. John Jr. was born in 1716 and was, by all accounts, the apple of his parents' eye. It is believed that John Jr. was a colicky child, prompting the Wyatts to move the nursery across the hall to a bigger room so that Beth would be able to sleep close to her beloved son. This room was intended to be a bedroom for John Jr. when he was older or for another child of John and Beth's union. However, following the tragic death of John Jr., and the subsequent suicide of Beth Wyatt, this room—as did the house—remained empty for the remainder of John Wyatt's life.

"Their story is so sad," I said.

"Can we please just get this over with?" Miltos asked.

Kai had already finished scoping out the room, and when I walked in, he said, "Nothing here."

He was right. There was nothing to see. No secret rooms or closet doors to open. I looked out the window overlooking the side of the house. Below was Sam's air mattress, on top of which was a neatly folded blanket, and a white trellis hung loosely against the exterior wall. I tried to imagine someone climbing up. The trip would have been treacherous, but doable.

"Good news, Miltos," I said. "I think we're done."

"Finally!" he said. "If we stay up here any longer, Beth Wyatt is sure to steal our souls."

As I walked out of the room, I said, "That trellis is barely holding together. Whoever it was *really* wanted to get into the house if they were willing to climb that thing to do it."

"The murderer isn't the only one who wanted to get into this house last night after we locked up," Miltos said.

"What do you mean?"

"Last night, Danny forgot something. His phone. He said he needed it and accidentally left it in the house."

I stopped walking. "Wait, I saw Danny put his phone in the lockbox with the rest of them this morning before we even got into the house."

"So?" he asked.

"I thought you said he forgot his phone."

"He said he did."

"Don't you think that's an important detail? Danny forgetting his phone?"

"Not really," Miltos said. "Danny always forgets his phone."

Seriously? I glanced at Kai, who was face-palming next to me.

"Yeah," I said, "but if Danny forgot his phone and really wanted it—so much so, that he asked about getting into Wyatt House after it was locked up for the night—wouldn't it be possible that the person we saw scaling the walls of Wyatt House on that video was Danny?"

Miltos blinked at me.

"And taking it a step further, if it *was* Danny, and he had gotten into the house, isn't it possible that he was the one who murdered Kai?"

"It couldn't have been Danny," Miltos said. "The person climbing the house was wearing a hat. Danny doesn't wear a hat."

Okay, this discussion was making me realize two things: 1) Danny was now a suspect in the murder of Kai Teller, and 2) Miltos was totally *not* a suspect. If he was having a hard time figuring out the connection I was presenting to him, then there was no way he would be able to get into Wyatt House, murder Kai, get out of the house without being seen, and play it off so expertly. I was surprised Kai had even put Miltos in charge of snacks.

"Anyway," Miltos said, "why would Danny want to murder Kai? They were best friends."

"You were ready to believe Sam murdered Kai, weren't you?" I asked.

"That was different. Her hat was found upstairs." He thought for a moment, and his eyes opened wide. "Unless ... do you think Danny could have put on Sam's hat, scaled the outside of the house, murdered Kai, and then left Sam's hat to try to incriminate Sam?"

Better late than never. "It's a possibility."

"But why?"

"I'm not surprised he doesn't remember," Kai said.

"Remember what?" I asked before I could stop myself.

Miltos looked at me strangely. "You're doing it again, you know. Talking to yourself. It's not a good look."

"Ask Miltos if anything happened between me and Danny right before we got to Wyatt House," Kai said.

"Miltos, did anything happen between Danny and Kai before they got to Wyatt House last night?" I asked.

"Oh, yeah. They had a big fight."

I stared at him. "Care to elaborate?"

"Danny found out about the surprise ancestry show Kai was planning to run."

"So, Danny knew about it? And told you?"

Miltos nodded.

"What about Sam and Justin? Did *they* know? Sam looked genuinely surprised."

Miltos shrugged. "I just knew about Danny and me."

"How did Danny find out?"

"I don't know. He didn't say. But he was pretty ticked off. He said friends didn't do that to friends."

I had to agree. "What did Kai say?"

"Why don't you just ask *me* what I said?" Kai asked me. He crossed his gray, ghostly arms.

"Kai told him to calm down," Miltos continued. "That it wasn't a big deal. Just a stupid prank. And then Kai said not to worry, when it came to skeletons in the closet, Danny's weren't as bad as some of the others."

"Meaning who?"

Miltos shrugged. "Probably me. My grandfather was a local celebrity in Greece before he came to the States. Yes, yes, I know, Greeks are known for many accomplishments. We rocked medicine, democracy, math, architecture—just to name a few things." He smiled, clearly proud. "But my grandfather was not a kind man—especially not to animals. There's old documentary footage of him doing some bad things, and I'm guessing that Kai found it and was going to talk about it."

"Oh, yeah!" Kai cheered.

"That's what Kai does," Miltos said. "He finds that little chink in your armor and sticks the point of his sword right through it."

"That's not very nice." I glanced at Kai.

"He doesn't do it to be mean," Miltos said.

"Thank you, Miltos," Kai said.

"He does it for the shock value. For the *likes*. The problem is, he doesn't think about how what he does affects everyone else."

Wow, that was pretty insightful for a guy who, three minutes ago, couldn't put two and two together. My estimation of Miltos was changing. I should have known better than to judge him so quickly. He gave Kai a lot of credit—maybe too much credit—but he accepted Kai for who he was, and that was pretty cool. Not many people I had come across did that. William came to mind.

Kai, suddenly, was quiet. I wondered if he was thinking about what Miltos had said. Was he harboring any guilt? It would have been admirable, but unfortunately, Kai's reckoning would come too late to correct any of his wrongs.

"Even so, man, Danny was not happy," Miltos said. "I'm not sure what kinds of embarrassing secrets he has in his past, but he stormed out of here last night. And that's probably why he forgot his phone."

That's right. I had bumped into Danny as he was leaving. He seemed so focused.

Danny was the murderer?

How ironic.

Miltos had been so concerned about coming face-to-face with a murderer on the second floor of Wyatt House. Meanwhile, he had possibly been best friends with one his whole life.

Chapter 12

"You have to say something, Miltos," I said.

"Me? Why *me*?"

"You're Kai's friend. Don't you want to get to the bottom of what happened? Danny might be Kai's murderer because of the information Kai's tell-all web show might have said about his family."

"Hey, Freaky Friday, did you find anything?!"

Ugh. The only thing uglier than learning that Kai was exposing all of his friends' secrets was having to be anywhere near Taylor.

"Hey, we have something," Taylor said, walking toward us with Danny. "You?"

I couldn't stop staring at Danny. *Is that what a murderer looks like?* I glanced at Miltos. He was staring at Danny, too.

"What's wrong, Miltos?" Danny asked. "It looks like you've seen a ghost."

Nope. Just me.

"Danny, I told her." Miltos pointed at me.

"Told her what?"

"That you wanted to get into the house last night because you forgot your phone." He shrugged his shoulders.

Taylor's body language changed. "You forgot your phone?" he asked Danny, taking a step away from him.

"I thought I did," Danny said. "But I made a mistake. I didn't leave my phone here. I left it in the car. I found it on the floor of the driver's seat."

"A likely story," Kai said.

"Or, maybe you climbed into the house to get it last night," Taylor said.

"*Or*, I didn't." Danny folded his arms.

"Or, you *did*, which gave you the opportunity to kill Kai." Taylor pulled out his little notebook from his pocket.

"What are you doing?" Danny asked.

"Getting this down. I'm writing down how all the suspects are connected to Kai Teller. Their opportunities and motives."

"But I don't have a motive. Why would I want to do anything to Kai?"

Kai tried to nudge Miltos, but his hand went right through Miltos's shoulder. But suddenly Miltos cleared his throat. "Because, maybe, you were mad about that family history web show Kai did on all of us?"

Danny leered at Miltos. "What are you saying, Miltos?"

"I'm not saying anything!" Miltos whined. "It was *her*." He pointed to me. "She's putting words in my mouth."

Taylor and Danny looked at me.

"Listen," I said, "I don't know you guys, and I don't know anything about detective work..."

"That's for sure," Taylor said, scribbling some more in his notebook.

"But whoever killed Kai had the means and a motive. Based on what Miltos just told me—"

"She made me, Danny," Miltos whined.

"You had both, Danny," I said. "Means. A way to get into the house. And motive. A reason to want to do Kai harm."

"You seriously think, Miltos, that I would kill Kai because of a stupid web show?" Danny asked.

"You were angry."

"Duh. I mean, my best friend in the world tricked me into handing him my DNA, all so he could find out family secrets and expose them to the world. It's not really the kind of happy memory that goes into a best man's wedding toast, is it?"

"What did he find out?" Miltos asked.

"Oh, it's good," Kai said to me.

Danny exhaled heavily. "He found out I was adopted, all right?"

"You were adopted?" Miltos asked, surprised. "You mean, Mama Jackman isn't your real mom?"

"She *is* my real mom, Miltos. As far as I'm concerned. She and my dad took care of me for my whole life. Gave me the best home. My childhood was the *best*. You hear me? The best. And I've known for years that I was adopted. She told me when I was a teenager. She said she didn't want to keep such a big secret. I appreciated that, but I told her I loved her and nothing would change that and that I had no desire to find my birth parents."

"For real?" Miltos asked.

"Yeah. You and Kai may find this hard to believe, but I'm cool with the way things are. I don't need to go looking for anyone. And we definitely don't need to be *telling* anyone about this. It's *our* business. But then Kai has to go and do this stupid family secrets show, or whatever he was calling it. And I thought, great, now everyone will know I was adopted." Danny blinked away some wetness in his eyes. "I didn't want to do that to my mom. She didn't deserve that. She didn't deserve people questioning her or us or whispering behind her back. Kai was my best friend, but he could be such a jerk."

"Yo, Danny, it was just for fun, man," Kai said, seemingly without any remorse. I could never understand why some people had no empathy or thought anything was fair game to get likes or subscribers. Not everything was about fame.

"That's touching and all," Taylor said, although I was pretty sure he didn't find it touching. "I hate to be the one to say it, but you're just proving Miltos's case."

"It's not *my* case," Miltos said. "It's hers." He pointed again to me.

"You have a motive," Taylor said to Danny.

"Not really. I didn't realize that Kai was keeping this project top secret and that only *he* had access to the information."

"But what if you *had* known?" I asked. "What if you had known that getting rid of Kai meant getting rid of this special-edition family-history show?"

Danny thought for a moment and then shook his head. "Sorry to disappoint all of you, but my mother taught me better than that. Killing is a sin."

"Hey!"

Sam and Vince came toward us, with Justin behind them, his camera phone still in his hands. "We didn't find anything," Sam said. "Did you?"

Taylor, Danny, Miltos, and I looked at one another.

"What is it?" Sam asked.

I wasn't sure of what to say. If word about Danny's adoption was going to get out, it should come from him. Not me. It was his story to tell. And certainly not Kai's.

But Danny didn't say anything. Instead, he pulled something out of his pocket. It was a ticket stub. "We found this," he said, "on the floor in the back room."

"I almost forgot," Taylor said, slipping his notebook into his pocket. "I got distracted by the news about *you*, Danny."

"What news about Danny?" Sam asked.

"What is *that*?" I pointed to what was in Danny's hand, and he held it up. A white ticket stub that was creased and looked like it had been through the wash a few times. The black lettering was faded but still legible. It read *Dave Matthews Band* and gave last weekend's date for a concert that took place at the Burroughs Theater in Salem.

The Dave Matthews Band?

I glanced at the illustration of Dave Matthews on Vince's shirt just as Justin zoomed his camera onto the stub and then the shirt. Wait ... *Vince* had killed Kai?

"Get that thing away from me." Vince swatted at Justin's phone. "Why are you all looking at me?"

"Why do you think?" Danny asked, holding up the ticket stub. "I found this upstairs."

"It's pretty incriminating," Sam said. "What would your ticket stub be doing up here unless you were on this floor before now?"

"That ticket stub isn't mine." Vince tried to grab it, but Danny pulled it away. "Let me read it." Danny held the ticket stub in front of Vince's face. "See? I had better seats than that. Just check my Insta. This isn't my ticket. And why would I kill Kai Teller? I'm a longtime member of the Kai Krew. I love his show. Why would I want to see him dead?"

I watched him closely, and while something told me he was telling the truth, his cheeks were flushed, his forehead wet, and his mouth twitchy. Definite signs of deception. But couldn't that happen to anybody accused of something they didn't do?

Suddenly, Taylor and Danny nodded at one another and grabbed Vince's arms.

"Hey, what are you doing?!" Vince exclaimed.

"Listen," Taylor said. "I don't know what motive you could have had, but this is pretty concrete evidence."

"Is it any more concrete than finding Sam's baseball cap up here?!" Vince shouted.

"What is going on up there?!" Stephanie yelled from somewhere below.

"I didn't put my hat up here!" Sam said.

"Oh, and we're just supposed to believe you?" Vince said.

"What about Danny's argument with Kai?" I asked.

"What was this argument between you and Kai about, Danny?" Sam asked.

"It doesn't matter," Taylor said. "Listen, you're *all* suspects. And that's why we're going to let the police handle it from here."

"Get your hands off me!" Vince roared as Danny and Taylor walked him toward the staircase, followed by Sam, Miltos, and Justin. I stayed back so that I could whisper to Kai.

"Do you know Vince?" I asked.

Kai shook his head. "Never saw him before in my life. And I would remember that red hair." He looked at mine. "No offense."

"So, he wasn't in any way involved in that stupid surprise family-history episode you were planning?"

"Um, it wasn't stupid. It was awesome. And, no, he wasn't. I *told* you. I've never seen him before."

Kai appeared genuine. And I assumed he would say if he knew Vince and would want to get to the bottom of his murder. I hurried to the rest of the group.

Downstairs, Linda was sitting on the floor next to Kai's air mattress. Stephanie and Alice were off to the side, also sitting on the floor with their backs to the wall. When Danny and Taylor strong-armed Vince down the stairs, they all stood up.

"What's going on?" Linda asked.

"We found a ticket stub for last week's Dave Matthews concert upstairs," Danny said, pulling on Vince's arm. "This guy went to that concert. He told us earlier today."

Linda glared at Vince. "You killed my baby?" she asked. Her hands balled into fists.

"No!" Vince's face, red from exertion, turned pale. "I didn't hurt anybody! I loved your son's show. And I would never hurt him. Hurt *you*. That's not my ticket stub."

"I don't know, guys," Miltos said. "Redheads aren't known to be vicious killers."

"Um, Miltos, that's totally not true," Danny said. "But why should I even listen to what you say? You think *I* killed Kai?"

"Why would *you* kill Kai, Danny?" Linda asked.

"Because of Kai's stupid family history show. Or whatever you're calling it," Miltos said as Justin zoomed the camera into his face. "Justin, put the camera down!"

"I'm calling the cops," Linda said.

Stephanie threw up her hands in victory. "Finally!"

"That's a solid lead." Linda was still glaring at Vince. "One of several, it appears. Thank you, everyone, for your help. I know many of you didn't agree with the decision to delay contacting law enforcement, but now that we've got suspects and are pretty sure the ghost of Beth Wyatt didn't kill my son, we can be sure that Feeding Salem will get its money. Miltos, help Danny and the reporter keep *the killer* secure."

"Me?" Miltos asked, surprised.

I agreed. Miltos could barely take care of himself, let alone bully Vince around, but suddenly Vince seemed to settle down.

"Yes, let's call the police," Vince said. "Then maybe finally you'll see that you're all off your rockers." He pulled his arms away from Danny and Taylor and sat on one of the wainscot chests at the side of the room, leaning back against the faded wallpaper.

"It's not that easy," Taylor said to Linda as he, Miltos, and Danny surrounded Vince like sentries. "There's gotta be a trial. Charges made."

"Maybe so." Linda punched 9-1-1 into her phone. "But as long as it looks like a ghost didn't kill my son from the get-go, then the donations go where they need to go—at least, initially—and that's all I care about. Because that's all my son cared about." She turned toward Vince. "And then we'll focus on making sure you pay for what you did and get what you deserve." She paused and lifted the bottom of her phone to her mouth. "Hello, this is Linda Teller. I'm at Wyatt House in Salem, Massachusetts. And I need help. My son has been murdered."

Chapter 13

"Kai! Kai! Kai!"

The chanting outside continued, although less excited and more impatient than before. I envied the members of the Kai Krew. I may have had posters of my favorite TV stars adorning my walls growing up, but I'm not sure I was so passionate about them that I would sleep in the street all night in support. I didn't want to think about what would happen when the front door to Wyatt House opened and Kai Teller didn't emerge. His superfans, up to this point, had been patient, polite, and understanding, but there was no telling how they would be with the news of Kai's demise.

"You have the wrong person. You realize that," Vince was saying, but no one was listening to him.

Except me.

I believed him.

I looked around for Kai and found him standing near his mother, who was staring down at his dead body. I hadn't noticed it before, but Kai and Linda resembled one another. A strong chin. High cheekbones. A lean frame. And they had an overall arrogance about them that reminded me somewhat of Joe. *Where does that come from?* Were you born with arrogance? Had it been passed down to Linda from one of her conceited parents and slipped to Kai through her narcissistic placenta? I looked at Vince. Linda had just accused him of murder, and yet he *still* gazed at her with adoration.

I tried to get Kai's attention without alerting the others. I cleared my throat a few times, which didn't work and only seemed to draw the attention of the one person I was trying to avoid. Taylor.

Before Taylor could say something snarky, I eased myself toward Linda as she watched Kai's still body on the air mattress. When she bent down to smooth out his blanket, I whispered to Kai, "I need to talk with you."

"So, go ahead," Kai said. "Talk."

Not the answer I was hoping for.

"Not here," I whispered into my hand, but Linda looked my way, and I launched into what I hoped was a believable coughing fit.

"Are you okay?" she asked.

I coughed a few more times for good measure before clearing my throat. "I think I just need to step into the bathroom for a minute."

"The bathroom doesn't work, honey," Linda said impatiently. "As soon as the police are here, you'll be able to go outside to the porta-potty."

"I just need to splash some cold water on my face."

"The plumbing doesn't work, either," Taylor said, even though no one was talking to him.

Ugh. I didn't think this would be so hard. I picked up a water bottle from Kai's snack table. "I'll use this." *Be assertive.* "And I'll be right back." I glanced at Kai, hoping he got the hint, and marched into the bathroom. When I turned to close the door, I breathed a sigh of relief when I saw him following me and closed the door behind him.

"That water bottle you took could have been evidence!" Taylor shouted as if he hadn't spent the previous half hour rummaging around upstairs and sprinkling his DNA all over the house. "Don't touch anything else!"

"Yo, that guy is a jerk," Kai said.

"Yeah, well, that seems to be the overwhelming opinion among the living *and* the dead," I said.

"So, why are we in here?" Kai asked, looking around the small bathroom.

"I don't know. Something doesn't seem right to me about accusing that Vince guy."

"You don't think he killed me?" Kai said. "Wow, I never thought I'd say those words together in a sentence."

"I don't think so."

"Why not?"

I shrugged. "A gut feeling, maybe? You're going to find this surprising, but this is not my first experience with a murdered ghost."

"Surprisingly, I don't find that surprising. Maybe I would have yesterday, but," he raised his gray, ghostly arms, "there's been a serious plot twist to my life. Or death. Or whatever." He looked at me with his piercing gray eyes. I couldn't remember what color they had been before.

Knock knock ...

Someone was rapping on the bathroom door. The sound was soft, which told me right away that

Taylor Hampton wasn't on the other side. I didn't take him for a soft knocker. "Yes?" I said.

"Are you all right in there?" Stephanie asked.

"Yes. I just need a few more minutes." I looked at Kai and whispered, "I guess I have to make this look good." I opened the water bottle, poured some water onto my fingers, and put dots of water on my forehead. "Do I look refreshed?"

"No, you just look wet," he said.

"Great, thanks." I reached for a paper towel, dried my hands, and was about to toss it into the garbage pail but stopped.

"What's the matter?" Kai asked.

Inside the pail was a chewed-on lollipop stick.

"There's a chewed-up lollipop stick in there," I said.

"So? Have you *met* Justin? There are chewed-up lollipop sticks *everywhere* Justin goes. It's like his calling card. Stuff just falls out of his pocket—and sometimes his mouth—on a regular basis."

"Yeah, but you don't understand. I was the last one in the bathroom last night. And I was going to toss in some trash but changed my mind because the garbage bag was clean and empty, and I didn't want to be the one to dirty it."

"I don't understand," Kai said.

"I'm saying that if it was clean last night, then it should be clean now. As far as I know, nobody else was in here since last night." I thought about it. "Unless Stephanie, Alice, or Linda came in here while we were upstairs, but why would they put a lollipop stick in the garbage?"

"Maybe to incriminate Justin?"

Possibly. "I'm pretty sure Alice and Stephanie wouldn't have. That leaves your mom."

"My mom did *not* kill me. C'mon, you can't seriously believe that."

"Like you said, plot twist."

More knocking on the door. "Clara, are you sure you're okay?" Stephanie again.

"Yeah, I'm coming out. Wait, Stephanie, can I ask a question?"

"Sure, what is it?" she said through the door.

"Did any of you come into this room while we were upstairs before? You, Linda, or Alice?"

"No, why?"

"No reason," I said. "I'll be out soon."

"See?" Kai said. "I told you. My mom didn't do this."

"Well, then ... that leaves Justin." A jolt of electricity ran through me. "He must have been in the house last night. Oh my God, *he* must be the one scaling the side of the house on that video, wearing Sam's hat to try to incriminate her. *He* must be the one who ... murdered you."

"Seriously? You think, after killing me, he came into the bathroom to gaze at his murderous reflection in the mirror, and then the lollipop stick just fell into the garbage?"

"I don't know. You said it yourself. He's always dropping things. Maybe he came in here to think. To catch his breath. Maybe the stick fell in there. Or he threw it into the garbage out of habit." My pulse quickened. "Or maybe he tossed it in without a care because there would be no way to prove the stick *wasn't* in there before last night. Who notices what's in a garbage pail anyway? He didn't count on *me*. I *know* that the garbage pail was empty."

"Um, did you take a photo of the garbage pail?" Kai asked.

What was it with these young people and taking photos of everything? "Of course not."

"Well, then you can't *prove* the garbage pail was empty. Anyway, Justin? Do you really think Justin could pull this off? And why would he?"

"*You* tell *me*. You know him better than I do."

"Justin is ..." Kai took one of those deep breaths that wasn't a breath at all. "How should I put this? Not the swiftest person on the planet. He's somewhere between a Danny and a Miltos—but closer to Miltos. He has this grand idea that he's going to be a YouTube star one day."

"He told me last night that he was putting together his own YouTube show and that you were supportive. We've already established that you weren't going to put him on camera for your own show, so I guess Justin having his own show was your way of getting him out of your hair?"

"Justin was never going to have his own show," Kai said flatly.

"What do you mean?"

"That's what I'm telling you." He pointed to his head. "Not much going on up here with that guy. Justin signed a non-compete when he joined my company. I told him that. He doesn't listen. There was never going to be a *Just Justin* web show. Not as long as ..." Kai paused, and his eyes opened wide.

"As long as you were alive," I finished.

"Wait, when did Justin mention the web show to you?" Kai asked.

"Last night. Right after he took my sponsor video."

"So, you think he planned this? He planned to kill me? *Here?*" He gestured around the small bathroom. "In this haunted house?"

"Very possible. Maybe he didn't *forget* about the non-compete at all. Maybe he thought if you were never going to give him a chance to be on screen more often and he couldn't have his own show, then his only option would be to get rid of you."

"That's insane," Kai said. "People don't get what they want, and they jump to violence?"

"Not all people. Just some." *Like Joe.*

"Why didn't I see it? I should have known. If I hadn't been focused on the family history show, maybe I would have realized Justin was up to something."

"Can I ask you a question?"

"Sure," Kai said.

"Did you really con your friends into giving you a DNA sample?"

"Pretty genius, don't you think?"

There was that arrogance again.

"I was calling the show 'A Deep Dive on the Kai Five,'" Kai said. "Clever, right? Who doesn't love alliteration and rhymes?"

"To be honest, I think it's a pretty despicable thing to do to your friends."

"Oh, c'mon. It's not a big deal. So what if I revealed some family history drama? You wouldn't believe the stuff you can find out from some spit."

"Like the fact that Danny was adopted."

"Danny's adoption?" He waved a dismissive hand. "No big deal. Did you know Justin's great-grandfather was a Nazi?"

Another jolt of electricity shot through me. "A Nazi?"

"Yeah. Crazy, right?"

"Yeah, and that wasn't something most people would want public," I said. "Do you know what that kind of information would do to Justin's brand if he tried to start a web show?"

"I told you. He wasn't starting any show."

"Whatever. But it would definitely make him angry. The question is, would it make him angry enough to kill you?"

Kai looked at me the way Joe used to. Like my logic wasn't adding up. "Not possible. Justin didn't know what I found out. I kept the findings of the show a secret."

"But what if he *did* find out?" I pressed.

"How could he?" Kai asked.

"In the envelopes that your mom left on the sponsors' tables was information on upcoming shows. Was there a reference to the DNA show in those? What if Justin saw what was inside the envelope? Then he would know what you were planning and what you found."

"I guess it's possible," Kai conceded. "But how would we know that? We can't just ask him if he went peeking into the sponsor envelopes. Or, at least, *I* can't."

"Wait, I think I might have proof!" The Polaroid picture. The one Stephanie had taken of me last night at my sponsor table. Justin was in the background. What had he been doing? I couldn't remember. I reached for my purse but realized I didn't have it. "Where's my purse?" I said frantically.

"I don't know. Don't look at *me*." Kai held up his hands.

Where can it be? And then I remembered. I placed it on the floor in the primary bedroom upstairs when I reached for the knitting needle.

"What is it?" Kai asked.

"I gotta go," I said and flung the bathroom door open.

Chapter 14

I dashed toward the staircase, my thoughts and body focused.

"Clara, what's the matter?" Stephanie called.

Don't stop. Keep running. "I need to get my purse. I left it upstairs."

"You shouldn't go up there," Taylor ordered. "The police are nearly here."

He was right. Other than the blood pumping through my ears, I could hear the faint sound of sirens coming from somewhere outside, but I kept running. If Taylor wanted to chase me down, let him.

When I got to the top of the staircase, I made a sharp right and headed for the master bedroom, leaping over the velvet rope. My purse was sitting on the floor, just where I left it. I opened it and rummaged around until I found the sponsor envelope I had placed inside it last night. I ripped open the seal and quickly scanned the marketing materials.

> *Opportunity of a lifetime!*
> *Get your brand in front of Kai's millions of followers!*
> *Millennials and Gen Z comprise the largest consumer demographic*
> *Blah blah*

Where was the info about the upcoming episodes of *Here Goes Nothing*?

Finally, I found it. Kai was planning to be buried alive, live in an igloo, fast for two days, and swim with sharks and a whole lot of other craziness during the rest of the year. But in a bold sidebar was an opportunity available only to current sponsors of the show: a special episode running on Monday that was predicted to be one of the most watched—if not *the* most watched—episodes of *Here Goes Nothing*'s run.

A Deep Dive of the Kai Five

This special episode of Here Goes Nothing *is history in the making and focuses on Kai's besties and most trusted advisers. You know them well. Linda. Sam. Justin. Danny. Miltos. The names roll off the tongue. The Kai Five, who work tirelessly behind the scenes. For one episode only, you'll get to learn all about them—and probably even more than you ever expected! This episode uncovers shocking revelations about their family histories. Who is a distant cousin of actor Keanu Reeves? Who was adopted as a baby after being discovered in a garbage dumpster? Who has thirteen sisters and brothers they didn't know about? Who has a high risk of developing Alzheimer's Disease? And whose family tree features a direct link to a Nazi—Heinrich Himmler, Reich Minister of the Interior under Hitler? "A Deep Dive of the Kai Five" will be the talk of the internet. Don't miss out! Sponsor this explosive episode today! (Note: as a past or current sponsor of* Here Goes Nothing, *you are bound by the terms of your sponsorship agreement from disclosing any and all information about upcoming episodes. Contract violations will result in either civil or criminal penalties.)*

Well, there it was in black and white. (Well, black and blue, which were Kai's brand colors.) A mention of the Nazi thing. But had Justin seen it?

I reached into my purse again and pulled out the Polaroid photo Stephanie had taken of me last night. My instinct was confirmed. 1) It was *still* one of the worst photos of me ever taken, and 2) there he was. Justin. In the background of the photo. And he was reading the contents of Alice's sponsor envelope.

He *knew* what was coming. How Kai was planning to ambush him and the others about their ancestry. *Motive.*

The chewed-up lollipop stick in the trash can. *Evidence.*

The desire to have his own web show, which was only possible upon Kai's death because of a non-compete clause. *Motive.*

A link to a notorious Nazi, which would possibly destroy any brand and goodwill he was trying to build. *Motive.*

Video of a person climbing the side of Wyatt House in the middle of the night. *Opportunity.*

Did I just solve the mystery?

"Clara!" Stephanie called.

I stepped out of the bedroom and glanced toward the stairway, but then my eye caught movement on the other side of the hallway. A door was softly closing. "Is there someone there?" I called.

No response.

I walked toward the top of the staircase. Downstairs, Justin was standing near Vince, watching over him as if he had absolutely nothing to hide. My eyes zeroed in on Vince's shirt. Dave Matthews Band. Something about it was niggling my brain.

Wait ... hadn't Justin mentioned, too, that he had seen the band in Salem? With some relative? On that same night? The ticket stub that Taylor and Danny found could very well have been Justin's, not Vince's, and fallen out of his pocket while he was making his getaway.

Creak ...

A noise. I looked across the hall. It was coming from the same room as the door that was ajar.

Was it the killer?

Had I been totally wrong? What if the killer—not Justin—really *was* up here and had somehow evaded us?

"Clara!" Stephanie called again. "The police are here!"

Before I could stop myself, I tiptoed away from the staircase toward the half-closed door. I stood before it and took a deep breath, kicking myself that I hadn't brought one of the knitting needles with me. Then I slowly pushed it open and found myself face-to-face with the ghost of Beth Wyatt.

Chapter 15

I was taken aback by her beauty, even in shades of gray. And her youth. She must have been in her late twenties. The same age as Kai and his cohorts. She had a round face, and her hair was high, almost like she was wearing a Bumpit. And it was braided in the back in a Princess Leia style—a look that was surprisingly modern. She was wearing a dark gray linen petticoat with stockings underneath.

Beth stared at me, her eyes wide. I didn't know what to do, so I stared back. I was used to ghosts chasing me down. Begging me to find their killers. But Beth Wyatt simply gazed at me with big, gray eyes.

Then, suddenly, she clenched her hands. And for a moment, I thought that Miltos had been right. That it hadn't been Justin who killed Kai, but Beth, whose gray hands had wrapped themselves tightly around his neck. If Beth had been haunting this old house since the eighteenth century, she definitely would have developed fine motor skills—just like William, who had figured out how to write with a ballpoint pen.

But Beth's hands weren't clamped in anger. More like uneasiness. She was watching me closely. And seemed more nervous than I was. Then suddenly she spoke.

"Why is everyone gathered here?" she asked. "'Tis never this noisy."

I didn't know what to say. "I'm sorry. It's a YouTuber...I mean, it's just a stunt, like a circus event."

"Who might you be?" she asked.

"My name is Clara Kelly. I live in Salem. Not far from here. I'm so sorry about the noise. And to have disturbed you."

And that's when I heard them. The sirens. The police were right outside the building.

But then I heard another sound. Clear as day.

Somewhere inside this old house, a baby was crying.

Chapter 16

Beth hurried past me out the door, gesturing that I should follow. She led me to the next room, which, according to the Salem Historical Society sign placed outside, was the nursery. Inside was a handcrafted wooden bassinet, one of the few pieces of furniture in the sparsely decorated room, and in it lay a beautiful gray baby boy, crying.

"There, there." Beth picked up the baby and nestled him against her breast. "Momma is here." She held him tightly, and within moments, the crying stopped. "He misses me when I depart." She looked at me warmly. "His name is John, after his father."

"He's very beautiful."

Beth beamed with pride. How content she looked. Not at all like the murderous, angry specter she was said to be. History had gotten her story wrong, just like it had gotten William's wrong. And I wondered in that moment if Beth Wyatt, after the criminal death of her child, had not taken her own life out of sadness but out of a sense of duty—a belief that, upon her death, she would go to whatever place came after life and care for her murdered boy. As I stood there, intruding on mother and child, it was comforting to know that the two of them would have each other for eternity.

I nodded as I took a step backward, not wanting to interfere any longer. Beth nodded back. And as I turned to go, she began to dance slowly, as if there were music playing, with the baby resting against her—the young woman who had wanted to be a dancer now dancing in perpetuity with her beloved child.

By the time I got downstairs, a bevy of police officers was filing through the front door and canvassing the first floor of Wyatt House, Officer Callahan among them. He was in the corner of the room, where Danny and Miltos were still holding Vince, and a few Emergency Medical Technicians were hovering over Kai's body.

Callahan was the last person I wanted to see. Especially around a dead body. How many times could this happen without him getting suspicious? And yet, as he questioned Vince, I knew I had to go up to him. I had to tell him I thought he had the wrong man.

I exhaled deeply and started to go, but then stopped.

There was another choice. And I couldn't believe I was considering it.

I searched the room until my eyes landed on Taylor Hampton, who was pointing out the choke marks on Kai Teller's body to the medical technicians. Arrogant, annoying Taylor. Did I really want to talk to that guy voluntarily? No. And yet I found myself taking a deep breath and, in one of those *never say never* moments, running toward him.

Chapter 17

Taylor stepped away from the EMTs—or, more accurately, had been shooed away—as I hurried toward him. I was about to call his name when someone touched my shoulder.

"Clara, here," Stephanie said, handing me my phone. "Finally, our phones are no longer being held hostage."

"Oh, great. Thank you, Stephanie."

She looked at me, concerned. "Are you okay?"

"Yeah, yeah, I just need to talk with Taylor."

"Why? I didn't think anybody wanted to talk to that guy."

"Yeah, I know." I smiled. "Trust me, I'm not thrilled about it."

"Well, I've already given a preliminary statement to one of the officers. It was pretty hard to explain how we could walk into Wyatt House at just before seven a.m. and only call the police a few minutes ago. But it is what it is." She shrugged. "Anyway, I'm going to head out. I think I've had my fill of death for a while. Hey, do you want to get together sometime? For coffee? Tea? And preferably in a place without ghosts or dead bodies?"

"I would like that." I nodded. "Should we invite Sebastian, too?"

"Nah." Stephanie waved a dismissive hand. "I'm pretty sure he wouldn't be interested in a threesome." She smiled. "Okay, great. See you soon, Clara."

"Bye."

As I watched her go, I couldn't help feeling that Stephanie had picked up on something between

Sebastian and me. Maybe more than I wanted to admit. Then I heard Officer Callahan say, "I'm *this close* to having you thrown out, Taylor."

Taylor must have made his way over to Callahan and was—not surprisingly—already bugging him in the several moments he had been there. Then Callahan turned and saw me, his eyes opening wide. Ugh. This was exactly what I had been trying to avoid. What was I going to say? *Yes, Officer Callahan, this marks the fourth time (if you include my husband) that you've seen me in the vicinity of a dead body.* But luckily Vince, who was being held by two officers—one of them I recognized as Officer Manning, Callahan's partner—began resisting, and Callahan turned away. Quickly taking advantage of my window, I punched a few buttons on my phone, which I stuck into my pocket, and walked up to Taylor, who was writing feverishly in his little notebook.

"Taylor, can I speak with you for a minute?"

"Now's not a good time, Freaky Friday. I've got to get this down before I forget it. I'm telling you, this article is writing itself."

Callahan was slipping handcuffs onto Vince, who continued to protest his innocence. I scanned the room. Linda and Kai's friends were all talking to the police or EMTs, including Justin, who kept glancing at Vince. I saw it now. Plain as day. The guilt on his face. It was amazing what you could see when you knew what to look for. I had to act fast.

"Taylor, I know who did it."

He didn't even look up. "You know who did what?"

"Seriously? You're not even going to look at me?" I lowered my voice. "I know who killed Kai Teller."

"So do we all, Clara. It was Vince. The guy from the comic book store. I'm telling you, you can't trust redheads." He glanced at my hair and smirked.

"Taylor, it wasn't Vince."

Finally, I got his attention. "Yes, it was."

"No. It wasn't."

He exhaled dramatically and wiped his bangs from his eyes. "Okay, then. Who was it?"

I crossed my arms. "I'll tell you. But on one condition."

"And what's that?"

"That you help me clear William Kensington's name."

"Who?"

"William Kensington. You know, the person who lived in my house back in the eighteen hundreds."

"The guy who was a traitor to his country that you want me to pretend was a hero so you can build a business? Yeah, right. No way."

"William Kensington *was* a hero. And, c'mon, it's easy for you to do a bit of research on it. You have access to the *Salem Chronicle* archives. There's probably a treasure trove of information there about the history of Salem. I'm sure that when you go through it, you'll see I'm right." *Well, eventually, I hoped he would.* "And you know what?"

Taylor sighed loudly. "What?"

"Not only will you become a hero for righting a longtime historical wrong, but you will be a hero when you solve this murder case for the Salem Police Department."

Taylor's eyelid twitched, and he didn't say anything. His eyes glazed over, like he was picturing himself accepting his good citizenship award for bringing down a cold-hearted murderer. The accolades. The adoration. Kai Teller and Taylor Hampton may have worked in different industries, but they were pretty similar when it came to their own narcissism.

"I'm reasonably sure you don't know what you're talking about and you're just trying to get me to build business for you, but go ahead. Tell me who *really* killed Kai Teller. Keep in mind, I'm not making any promises, okay? I'll do what I can to clear the name of this Kelvin fellow."

"William Kensington. And stop pretending you don't know his name."

"Right, William Kensington. How can I forget when you keep barking the name into my ear? Whatever. I'll do my best."

I knew *I'll do my best* was often code for *don't count on it*. Taylor was giving himself an out. I put my hands in my jacket pocket.

"I mean it, Taylor. I expect you to do a bit of digging. If I give you the name of the murderer of Kai Teller, will you help me track down the true history regarding the house I moved into, Kensington House? I have your word?"

"Are you deaf? I already said I would." Taylor put his hand on his chest as if he was about to recite the Pledge of Allegiance. "You have my word that I will investigate the history of William Kensington if you give the name of Kai Teller's killer."

"Yeah, well, I don't believe you." I pulled my phone out of my pocket and stopped the recorder app. "But I have you on audio that you'll do it. And maybe that's good enough to make you."

"You were recording me? Without my knowledge?"

"Yes. Pretty smart, huh?"

"More like pretty stupid." He smirked again. "Looks like *you* might be the one ending up in prison along with Comic Book Guy. Two gingers. Perfect."

"And why is that?" I asked, confused.

"Massachusetts is a two-party consent state. You can't record a conversation with me unless I agree to it. I can sue you."

Ugh. I really had to get my facts straight before I tried to extort someone. But I wasn't about to let Taylor think he had gotten one over on me. "Go ahead. Sue me. I just inherited a ginormous amount of money and I'm happy to go to court for a good cause. At that point, though, it might be too late."

"What do you mean?"

"Well, you know how it is. Photos. Audio. Video. It's all saved to the cloud, but things get leaked all the time. Who's to say the audio won't get leaked on the internet of me handing you Kai's killer and then you not following through on our deal? Your integrity will take a hit." I was pretty sure Taylor had *no* integrity to begin with. And I had no idea if things really got leaked from the cloud like raindrops. But it sounded good.

"Now you're blackmailing me?" he asked.

"C'mon, Taylor, I'm just asking for your help. You have everything to gain here. Fame. Fortune. Status. All I'm asking you to do is a little research on William Kensington. What do you say?"

Taylor seemed to be weighing his options. But what I said was true. He really had nothing to lose. Other than a few hours of his time. Finally, he threw up his hands. "All right, all right, I'll help you. I knew you were freaky, but you're kinda crazy, too, aren't you?"

"Let's go! We're clearing out this room!" Officer Callahan shouted as several detectives arrived, including Detective Daniels who had worked the Marlena Ryder case.

"Crazy as a fox, maybe," I said with a smile and then, as much as I couldn't believe what I was about to do, told Taylor Hampton everything.

Chapter 18

I stood in front of my sponsor table, watching Taylor speak to Officer Callahan. I didn't realize it would be such a spectacle. Taylor was gesticulating dramatically as if he were reenacting a scene from an *Avengers* movie. His hands were flying all over the place. He was ducking down as if dodging a sniper's bullet. And then he was pretending to climb, which must have been his way of replicating Justin scaling the side of Wyatt House. I had the urge to grab a tub of popcorn.

"This is quite possibly the *worst* sponsor table I've ever seen," Kai said, inspecting my mailing list. "You only have one name on here."

"Yeah, well, everyone has to begin somewhere," I said. "You didn't just have millions of subscribers when you started out, right?"

"I had *one*," Kai said. "My mom. She is my first and biggest fan." He glanced sadly at Linda, who was speaking to Detective Daniels over by Kai's air mattress. "I hope she'll be okay with me gone. It's been just the two of us for so long."

"I don't know your mother very well, Kai, but I get the impression she is very strong."

He nodded as I began packing up what little business materials I had. Officer Manning, who was standing at the front door, saw what I was doing and stepped toward me, holding up his hand. "Ms. Kelly, we'd like you to leave that for now. When we've gone over the crime scene, we'll contact you, and you can collect your things." He held open the front door.

"Oh, okay." I nodded, took one last look at Taylor and Callahan, and walked outside.

Throngs of people were still in the street. They were no longer chanting and, instead, had confused and anxious looks on their faces and their phone cameras in the air.

"*What's happening?*"

"*Where's Kai?*"

"*Why are the police here?*"

"*We deserve to know!*"

"*Did he get killed by a ghost?!*"

Sam was standing to the side of Wyatt House, alone, next to a table full of empty donut boxes imprinted with the *Haunted Cookie* logo. She was watching the crowd. I walked over to her, with Kai in tow. "You all right?" I asked.

She reached for the brim of her blue baseball cap that wasn't there. "The police bagged my baseball cap for evidence," she said. "Do you really think that red-headed Vince guy killed Kai and tried to frame me? It doesn't make sense."

I didn't know how much to say. If I told her what I knew, then I felt like I was reneging on the deal I had made with Taylor. *He* was supposed to be the one who figured out the truth. And save the day. Avenger-worthy. "I don't know," I said with a shrug. "For what it's worth, Sam, I never believed you were the murderer."

"Neither did I," Kai said, standing next to me.

"I appreciate that, Clara," Sam said. "I couldn't believe how quickly the others turned on me. I considered them friends. It was like *Lord of the Flies* and I was Piggy."

"People do all kinds of things when they're scared," I said.

"I actually have *you* to thank for my not being a suspect. If you hadn't had a stomachache or needed to use the bathroom last night, there would be no one to account for the fact that I left Wyatt House when I did."

"Three cheers for stress-related stomach pain, I guess." I smiled.

The front door to Wyatt House opened, and Linda Teller and a few police officers exited. The crowd began calling her name as the officers guided her toward an ambulance, where she spoke with another EMT.

"I don't think it's hit her yet," Sam said. "You know, that Kai is gone. Although it's kinda weird."

"What's weird?" I asked.

"Somehow, I feel like Kai's still here."

I glanced at Kai, who smiled.

"I wish I'd known how you felt about me," Kai said to Sam. He reached out to touch her shoulder, but his hand went right through it. "Maybe it would have changed things."

"I'll miss him," Sam said, "but, hey, at least my mom will be happy."

"She didn't like Kai?" I asked.

"No, she wanted me to go to med school. I guess that's where I'm headed."

A police officer nearby made space for a man to hop over one of the barricades controlling pedestrian traffic; he escorted him toward Wyatt House. The man had red hair and was thin, like Vince. He held in his hand what looked like a ticket stub and some kind of paperwork.

"Who's that?" Sam asked.

"I don't know," I said. "But he looks a lot like Vince. Only younger. Maybe it's a brother?"

"I don't think I want to know." Sam stuck out her hand. "I'm done with social media and web shows and all this stuff. If all goes well, the only poking I'll be doing is with a stethoscope." She smiled. "Good luck to you, Clara. I hope your bed-and-breakfast is an amazing success."

"Best of luck to you, Sam." I shook her hand.

As Sam left, the front door to Wyatt House opened again, and Detective Daniels walked out, followed by Officer Callahan and Officer Manning, who had a handcuffed Justin walking between them. Justin wasn't protesting. In fact, there were tears coming down his cheeks. Had he confessed? Had he decided to go quietly? I wanted to tell him that it didn't matter who his great-grandfather was or associated with, that he wasn't responsible for his ancestors' behaviors. Just as William wasn't responsible for who his descendants came to be.

"Wow, it really was Justin, huh," Kai said, watching the officers place Justin in the back of a squad car; the crowd of onlookers jockeyed for position to get a good photo of him. How ironic that Justin was finally getting what he wanted—to be the center of attention and star of his own video.

"What's happening?" someone was shouting.

"Is that Justin?" called another.

"Are we going to get this show on the road?" a woman was asking, and I realized it was Mavis. She looked at her watch. "I have a hair appointment that I need to get to," she said to no one in particular.

The front door to Wyatt House opened again and out walked Vince Hughes with the other red-headed fellow. Vince looked at the crowd and shook his head. When he saw me, he walked in my direction.

"Well, this sponsorship didn't go the way I thought it would," he said, running his hand through his spiky red hair. "Thank God my brother found my ticket stub on my desk at the store with a bunch of other things I've pulled from my pockets in the last week. Who knew being a slob would keep me from being in the back of a police car?"

"Hi, I'm Ross, Vince's brother," Ross said to me.

"Clara," I said.

"Care to join us for something to eat?" Ross asked.

"After the morning I've had, I need to eat," Vince said. "A lot."

"Nah, I think I'm going to stick around a little bit," I said, taking a quick look at Kai. "Did Justin confess?"

"The kid folded like a house of cards once the detective applied a little pressure," Vince said. "I tried to tell these people there was no way I could scale a wall with my knee the way it is. But nobody wanted to listen." He glanced at Linda sitting on the edge of the ambulance. This time, the dreamy gleam in his eye was gone. "I guess things aren't always as they seem, right?" He shrugged. "Lesson learned. See you around, Clara."

As they walked away, Kai leaned toward me. "Did you see the way that guy was looking at you?" he asked.

"Who, Vince?"

"No, dummy. His brother. I think he likes you."

"He just met me," I said. "How could he like me?"

"Fine, don't believe me." Kai shrugged. "What do I know? I'm just a ghost."

Members of the crowd turned their attention from Justin to Detective Daniels, who was walking onto the small stage that had been set up in front of Wyatt House. Before getting into his squad car, Officer Callahan looked back at Daniels with a forlorn look in his eyes. Something told me that Callahan would have preferred to be the one standing on stage instead of driving away from the spotlight.

As Callahan and Manning left, Daniels was joined by Linda Teller and Taylor Hampton, who was waving to the crowd like a politician running for office. My guess was that Kai had been planning to stand on that stage as well, handing over a giant check to Feeding Salem. Unfortunately, the event had turned out much different from what he had planned. I glanced at the media presence at the back of the crowd. Those tech journalists were about to get a scoop they hadn't planned on.

"Good morning," Detective Daniels said, speaking into a microphone and tapping it with his forefinger.

"Where's Kai?" someone shouted.

"My name is Detective Daniels. I am a member of the Salem Police Department. I know you're here in support of Kai Teller, and I am here to tell you briefly what transpired today, and then I will hand the microphone over to Mrs. Linda Teller, whom I believe most of you are familiar with." Linda kept her eyes downcast, whereas Taylor was preening like a peacock beside her. "At approximately two a.m. this morning, Kai Teller was murdered while sleeping on the ground floor of the building you see behind me, known as Wyatt House."

Gasps emerged from the crowd. Followed by screams. And then a chorus of voices. The journalists, who had been standing in the back, pushed forward.

"It was the ghost!" someone shouted.

"Beth Wyatt killed our Kai!" called another.

Detective Daniels held up his hand.

"Justin Rubin has been arrested for the murder of Kai Teller. The department will provide more details at a later time, but we would like to take a moment to thank Taylor Hampton of the *Salem Chronicle*, who was instrumental in helping us solve this crime."

Taylor quickly muscled his way to the podium and took a quick bow. "It was my pleasure to help local law enforcement," he said into the microphone. "I should be thanking you for all you do. I am but a humble servant."

Oh, brother.

"Thank you, Taylor." As Detective Daniels politely motioned for him to step back, the crowd was stirring now, rocking into one another and looking dangerously close to becoming an angry mob. Linda grabbed the microphone and pulled it toward her.

"Please, everyone. Listen, please." She looked as if she was holding back tears. Kai stepped forward toward his mother. "You ... your support ... has meant everything to my son. Everything. This web show meant everything to him. I am here to tell you that we will be accomplishing what we set out to accomplish here. We will be donating one million dollars to the Feeding Salem charity. And that is because of *you*. *Your* donations. *Your* support. For years, Kai has done so many crazy stunts that I had sort of resigned myself to the fact that I might lose him one day. How many times can you tempt fate? Whether it was underground in New York City. On the plains of Nebraska during a storm. That time he did an overnight in an Icelandic ice cave. Each time I said goodbye to him, I knew there was a good chance that I may never see him again."

"We love you, Linda!" a young man in the crowd shouted.

"I love you, too. And so did Kai, who lost his life doing what he loved. I take great solace in that. We should all be so lucky to do in life what is our passion. Over these past few hours, I've thought very much about what to say to you this morning, following this unspeakable tragedy. And it's this: Kai would want you all to follow your own hearts and your own passions. Do what you love, what gives you pleasure. Our web show may be coming to an end …"

A collective "Nooooo!" emerged from the audience.

"But I promise you, I will continue Kai's work in supporting local charities across the country and the world. *That* is my passion as well. I refuse to let the bad in the world destroy the good."

Amen to that. I decided on the spot that I would donate to Feeding Salem as well. I wanted to do some good in the world with Joe's money. Feeding hungry families was a perfect place to start.

The crowd burst into applause as Linda Teller stepped down from the short stage and walked with Detective Daniels and Taylor toward one of the police cars. I was beginning to see what Vince Hughes had seen in her. She was an empathetic and exceptional speaker.

"I can't believe I'll never see her again," Kai said to me as the mass of people began to talk among themselves, record videos in front of Wyatt House, and disperse.

"I have a feeling you will one day." I fished around in my purse until I found my ear buds and placed them in my ears.

"What's that for?" Kai asked.

"Just a little trick I use to speak to the dead without attracting attention." Down the block, I saw Alice standing on the corner, watching. I waved, but she turned abruptly and hurried away. I knew she wasn't a people person, and with all that had happened that morning, I wouldn't have been surprised if Alice never wanted to leave her house again.

"So where are you off to?" Kai asked. "Heading home?"

"Yes, I can't wait." *Home.* With William, Boy, and Ghost Cat. It was a weird sensation to be homesick. I hadn't felt it in a long time. "But there's one stop I need to make first."

"I think it's time for me to go, too," Kai said. He lifted his hands, which were beginning to fade. "Thank you, Clara. For all your help."

"I guess you're off to your next stunt."

"Yeah." Kai shrugged. "Here goes nothing," he said and vanished.

I took a deep breath and looked at all of Kai's fans, so many of whom were crying and hugging one another. Kai was lucky in so many ways. Yes, he was arrogant, but he had the ferocious love of a mother.

The loyalty of friends—well, all except one. And the adoration of millions. All these people may not have really known him, but they did in their own way, and he made them happy.

    I looked up at the second floor of Wyatt House. Beth Wyatt was staring down at me, her baby in her arms. I smiled. She smiled back. And then I turned and walked toward downtown Salem and the family that was waiting for me.

Chapter 19

"Well, hello, Clara!" Mr. Wiggins was sitting in front of his house in a lawn chair, getting some sun, as I walked toward my driveway. "Beautiful day today."

"Indeed, it is. Don't forget the sunscreen, Mr. Wiggins."

"Yes. Always. Thirty SPF. Wouldn't leave home without it." He shifted in his chair. "Do you need help with those packages?"

I lifted the two bags I was carrying from the electronics store up and down like dumbbells. "No, I think I've got it. Building up my strength. Thank you, Mr. Wiggins."

"Oh, and Clara, you have a—"

"Hello there."

Allison was standing by my front door, her beady brown eyes scanning my face, then my body, then the bags in my hands. I felt like I had just walked through the security scanner at the airport.

"Yes," Mr. Wiggins chuckled, "you have a visitor."

"Duh, she sees that." Allison rolled her eyes.

How rude. I hoped Mr. Wiggins hadn't heard the comment, but he had lost most of his hearing in his left ear—not his right one, which was facing us. "What are you doing here, Allison?" I placed the bags on the ground.

"I came to give you one last chance to give up."

"Give up?"

"You know, on fighting me and my parents for this old house." She knocked on the building's brick face. "Yes, you inherited a lot of money from my brother—which is not rightfully yours, of course—but even so, it's not enough to fight me in court. Joe may have had money, but our parents have *money*. You can save yourself a bundle by just forgetting all about this court case. I'll even give you a nice stipend if you'll just agree to our demands. You can move back to your father's little house on Long Island. Start over."

I folded my arms. "I'm not leaving. Frankly, *you* should be the one leaving. This isn't your house. It's *mine*. For better or for worse. Why can't you see I've made a home here? I'm not bothering anyone. Just trying to find happiness again."

"As far as I'm concerned," Allison said, "you don't deserve to be happy ever again."

"I'd like you to leave, Allison. Or do I need to get a restraining order?"

"Fine." She walked past me, brushing me with her shoulder and stopping in front of Mr. Wiggins, who was folding up his chair, his good ear toward us. "By the way," she said to him. "I think you should know that your new neighbor is a total fake and liar. Her name isn't Clara. It's Emily. Emily Turner. Just ask her." Allison pointed at me and walked away triumphantly.

My body flooded with anxiety. The way it had after I recorded Kai Teller's sponsor video. I took a deep breath as Mr. Wiggins looked up at me with his compassionate face. *What would I say to him?* I didn't want to lie anymore, especially to sweet, old Mr. Wiggins who had been nothing but kind to me since I came here. I owed it to him to tell him everything. After all, if it weren't for him, I might very well be on trial right now for Joe's murder, a murder I didn't commit.

I cleared my throat. "Mr. Wiggins, I—"

Mr. Wiggins raised his crooked hand. "I believe it was Shakespeare who wrote, 'That which we call a rose, by any other word, would smell as sweet.'" He smiled and waddled his way to his doorstep, dragging his chair behind him and leaning it against the building. He looked at me. "We all deserve the chance to become who we were meant to be. A name is no different from clothing, really. It cloaks us. But it's not who we really are. We are who we are on the *inside*. That's all that matters." He nodded sweetly. "Have a good evening ... *Clara*."

Tears welled in the corners of my eyes. Mr. Wiggins accepted me as the person he knew. For the person I had shown him to be. It was the greatest gift anyone could have given me. I wanted to wrap him in a giant bear hug.

"Oh, dear me, I forgot," Mr. Wiggins said as he hobbled up the steps to his home. "Clara, you've got some mail there on your doorstep. Such a big box. I hope it's something special."

I looked at the package, which I hadn't noticed before. "It is, Mr. Wiggins. Thank you. Thank you for . . . well, everything."

"Have a good evening, my dear," he said and closed his door.

Chapter 20

I grabbed the box on my doorstep and, also juggling my two bags, unlocked the front door and hurried inside.

Bark!

Boy came charging toward me.

I placed everything on the floor and picked up that little black-and-white licking machine. "Oh, my sweetie, I feel like I haven't seen you in forever." Boy wiggled in my arms with happiness, dotting my face with kisses, as I spotted the wee-wee pad near the front door. "And you peed on the pad! What a good boy you are!" I smooshed his adorable face.

"How was your event?" William asked, appearing near the kitchen.

"You wouldn't believe me if I told you." I placed Boy on the floor and scratched his little head. "You must be so hungry, Boy. I'm sorry I'm so late."

"I've already tended to the dog's feeding," William said.

I looked up at William in surprise. "You have?"

"Indeed, I was reading in the parlor when he entered and fixed his gaze upon me. I made my way to the bookshelf, and he persisted in his watch. He followed me to the kitchen. For a creature lacking the gift of speech, he certainly makes his intentions known."

"That he does." I kissed Boy's little head.

"I prepared his meal, and it was devoured before I returned the box to the cupboard. Such a hearty appetite for so small a creature."

"Thank you, William. That was very kind of you to feed him."

"What might *that* be?" William pointed to the box.

"Ah yes." I picked up the box and packages from the floor and brought them to the dining table. "It's a surprise." I hurried into the kitchen, grabbed a pair of scissors, and slit the top of the box. A puff of cold air wafted into the room.

"Your cheeks are quite flushed," William said.

"Yes, it's a refrigerated package."

"Refrigerated?"

"Our appliances aren't coming until later in the week, but I didn't want to miss the day."

"The day?"

"Yes, today, William. June seventh. It's your birthday!" I opened the box and pulled out the six-inch rainbow-flecked birthday cake I had ordered. "It's called Party in a Box. Everything you need for a birthday celebration."

I quickly set the table. "I'll put out a plate for you, William. I know you can't eat anything, but everyone should have a birthday cake on their birthday. Even if it's for show."

I reached into the box and pulled out the two party hats that were included. I put one on my head and the other on Boy, who, surprisingly, didn't seem to mind.

"Oh, my gosh, you're so cute." I reached for my phone and snapped a photo of him. "Okay, next are the candles. How old would you be today?"

William thought for a moment. "One hundred ninety-nine."

"Wow," I said. "You've almost hit your bicentennial. That was a big deal, by the way, when the United States reached two hundred years. But I don't have two hundred candles, so we'll settle for just one." I placed it in the center of the cake. "Okay, I think that's everything. Oh, wait!" I reached into the box and took out the one piece of wrapping paper that came with it. Then I grabbed the bags on the dining table and ran into the living room.

"Where might you be headed?" William asked.

"Give me one minute!" I called as Boy came running after me, his pointy party hat bobbing up and down. After a few minutes, Boy and I returned, and I handed William the wrapped gift in my hand. "This is for you."

"I don't understand."

"It's your birthday present. Everyone should get a little something on their birthday. This is a gift from me to you."

"You procured me a *gift*?" He took the box into his hands. "What might it be?"

"It's a surprise, silly. I can't tell. Right, Boy?"

Bark!

I picked up Boy and sat with him at the table.

"What am I to do with it?" William asked.

"You open it! I hope you like it."

William placed the package on the table and fingered the paper.

"I only used one piece of tape," I said, "so it should be easy to open. No need to be so careful. That's the best part of getting a present. Ripping off the paper."

William slid his gray finger under the paper and gingerly unstuck the tape. When the paper fell open, he stared at the writing on the box. "Long battery life?" he asked.

"I got you your own phone!" I reached over and lifted the cover of the box, exposing the phone inside. "Do you like it? I bought it at the electronics store after my event, when I got my new laptop. And I made sure they set it all up for you, so we don't have to worry about any of that. Now you have complete access to the internet and everything you've ever wanted to know! You also have your own phone number, so you can text and call me whenever you like, if I'm not here. Like if you need to remind me to feed the dog." I laughed and kissed Boy's wet snout. "And last night, I signed you up for your own free email account. Now you have complete access to this world. Eventually, we'll have Wi-Fi in the house, but we don't have to get into that now. And there's a screen protector in case the phone falls onto the floor or a certain Ghost Cat decides to play with it."

As if on cue, Ghost Cat entered the room and casually sauntered toward the dining table. She sat down on the floor, gazing up curiously at Boy's party hat.

"Now you're a twenty-first century dude, William!" I said. "You can take photos. Email. Text. And swipe! Let's not forget swiping!"

William appeared overwhelmed, staring into the box. The color of his pale blue eyes deepened. He ran his hand along the phone's screen. "Clara, I am at a loss for words. This is more than generous."

"William, it pales in comparison to what you've done for me. And that's what friends do, right? We celebrate one another. Oh, and now's the best part."

"Is there yet more?" he asked.

"Yes!" I carried Boy to the antique cabinet and retrieved one of the old matchboxes from the drawer. I flicked off the light, lit the candle, and began to sing. "Happy birthday to you ..." I knew I was off-key—Joe used to tease me about my terrible singing voice—but I was hopeful William wouldn't notice. I bounced Boy on my knee, and the party hat fell over his eyes. I fixed it and continued. "Happy birthday to you! Happy birthday, dear William. Happy birthday to you!"

When I finished, William stood there, not knowing what to do.

"Okay, it's tradition that the birthday boy closes his eyes to make a wish and then blows out his candle," I said. "But since we can't do that, I thought maybe if we blew out the candle together, it would feel like you were really blowing out your own candle. Sound good?"

"All right." William nodded. "Now?"

"Whenever you're ready."

William closed his eyes for a long moment. When he finally opened them, he looked at me as if to make sure he had done everything right.

"You made your wish?" I asked.

"Yes. Must I say what I wished for?"

"No, wishes are usually secrets," I said, even though I was *dying* to know.

"Clara, if you are to extinguish the candle with me, you ought to make a wish as well."

"You really think so? But my birthday isn't until next February."

"I think it only proper."

I looked at Boy. "What do *you* think? Should I make a wish?"

Bark!

"Ghost Cat, are you in agreement?"

She blinked at me.

"I'll take that as a yes. All right then. Let me think." I closed my eyes and thought of Boy in his cute party hat, of Ghost Cat, who was probably licking her paw in boredom, and William, who couldn't stop gazing at his new phone. Then I pretended to make a wish. For William's sake. Because, in truth, I really didn't have to.

All my wishes had already come true.

Want more Clara and William? Claim your copy of *Anything Ghost*, Book 4 in the Salem Spirits Cozy Mysteries series, and read how their story continues!

Sign up for Dina Marie's email newsletter and get a Salem Spirits Cozy Mysteries short story for free! Yes, free! Visit dinamariebooks.com for details.

About the Author

Dina Marie is the pen name of award-winning novelist Dina Santorelli, who has been obsessed with all things ghost since . . . well, forever. Married on Halloween, she likes vacationing in spooky cities and visiting cemeteries  and haunted hotels. A recent visit to Salem, Massachusetts, inspired her Salem Spirits series, which she wrote, in part, for her mom, a lover of cozy mystery TV.

Made in the USA
Middletown, DE
12 September 2025

17522352R00159